Whom Shall I Marry ...
An Earl or A Duke?

Whom Shall I Marry ... An Earl or A Duke?

Laura A. Barnes

Laura A. Barnes
2019

First Printing: 2019
ISBN: 978-1074406578
Laura A. Barnes

www.lauraabarnes.com

Cover Art by Cheeky Covers
Editor: Polgarus Studios

To my family
Thank you for all your love & support

Prologue

Sophia wandered around the luxurious parlor, feeling an odd sense of comfort. Why was she so relaxed in a house of ill-repute? Her fingertips traced across the fireplace mantel, caressing the smooth finish. The room displayed an elegance, the kind one would find in the grandest homes in Mayfair. However, she wasn't in Mayfair. She was inside a brothel in Vauxhall Gardens. Why she allowed her best friend Lady Sidney Hartridge to persuade her to come here was lost on her at the moment.

Belle, the madame of the brothel, ushered Sidney into a private chamber. Once she returned, Belle held out a mask for Sophia to wear. It was a delicate design in a turquoise color decorated with sequins adorning the sides. The mask covered her face securely, only allowing her lips to show. She had to unwind her hair and drape her blonde tresses across her shoulders. Belle helped to tie the ribbon behind her head. She informed Sophia that she didn't want to risk exposing her to any of her customers. The repercussions would cause Belle to lose clientele. Also, Sophia's reputation would be ruined.

Sophia again strolled around the room, impatient for Sidney to return. What was taking her so long? She knew Sidney's experiment on exposing the gentlemen of the ton to their unsavory behavior would get them into trouble. She proved to be correct once again. Sidney always jumped feet-first into strife, while Sophia was one to proceed with caution. However, now they were beyond caution and in danger of ruination.

The fire in the parlor was too warm for Sophia. Her discomfort was a result of her nerves being on edge about getting caught. Since she was in a private room where only Madame Belle could enter, she decided to get more comfortable. She undid the first few buttons and opened her dress wider. When that didn't cool her off, she loosened the strings on her chemise. While her breasts were not exposed, they were revealed in an inappropriate manner. Wanting a breath of fresh air, she went to where a breeze slipped through the window cracks. She pressed her head against the cool pane, seeking relief. Sophia took a few deep breaths as she tried to calm herself. Closing her eyes, her body relaxed, only to turn tense again as she heard the opening click of the door. She gasped in embarrassment, then realized the only people who would come into the parlor would be Madame Bellerose or Sidney. Finally, they could leave, and nobody would be the wiser of their visit.

When Sophia turned toward the door, her relief changed to fear. It wasn't Belle or Sidney that stood before her, but none other than Alexander Langley, the Duke of Sheffield. Her eyes widened in fright at her unfortunate luck. How would she remove herself from this predicament? He would ruin her, rather than save her. Her hatred of this man knew no bounds. His overbearing attitude regarding Sidney fueled her anger toward him. She pressed herself against the window, hoping to hide between the drapes. However, he was already aware of her. He froze Sophia in place with his gaze of desire.

Alex closed the door and leaned against the panel as he stared at the most amazing creature before his eyes. A new courtesan, no doubt. The mask she wore hid her identity, yet failed utterly to disguise her beauty. If he was a naïve young man, he would say she appeared frightened. But considering where they were, he knew it must be an act she tried to portray. While her eyes may speak fear, her body screamed siren. Her curly blonde hair lay tousled around her shoulders, her lips full and pouty, begging for someone to kiss them. Mmm, well he would have to change that shortly. Her simple dress suggested an innocent virgin. However, the undone buttons teasing him with the display of her breasts showed the role she performed. He never enjoyed these acts of play. Perhaps, he was missing out. He couldn't lift his gaze away from her chest. In fact, it was what drew him closer to her. The need to touch her.

His footsteps brought him but an inch away from her. He heard the hitch in her breath at his closeness. When his fingers hovered over her creamy flesh, she let out a gasp. He felt the heat singe him and he stilled. Alex was in awe of the effect she held over him. He had yet to caress her, but she already felt like heaven to him. His fingers trailed across her chest. Her skin was the softest silk, smooth, and pleasurable to his senses. He began to explore her hidden charms as his fingers dipped inside her chemise. When his touch brushed across her nipples, they contracted into tight buds. He lowered his head, lost in a sensual desire, and a moment later she pulled out of his grasp.

Alex shook his head to clear his mind. A courtesan never affected him this strongly. He must pull himself together or she would take advantage of him. A duke must always be in control, even in the height of passion. If not, he was nothing but a mere man. And the Duke of Sheffield was anything but a mere man.

Sophia stood in shock. Did the Duke of Sheffield actually place his hands on her breasts and fondle her? The more important question was why she hadn't stopped him? He caught her unaware with the feelings he ignited in her. They were new to her. How did a man she detested awake her sexual awareness?

He watched the confusion in her eyes. They were a magnificent violet. Violet? Were her eyes the shade of purple? He peered into them, lost in her gaze, and admired the beautiful colors as they changed to match her emotions. When Alex again tried to close the gap between them, she slid past him to make her way behind a chair. So, this was how she would play this game. She was intriguing enough that he allowed himself to indulge her.

"Belle had not informed me of a new girl. What is your name, my darling?"

Sophia shook her head in denial. She couldn't speak without Sheffield recognizing her voice. She was caught in his trap until Belle rescued her. Sophia couldn't simply escape either. It risked running into another member of the ton. She was stuck in this intimate room with the one man she disliked above all others.

"Mmm, you wish to remain mysterious. I am game. It has been a long while since any woman has drawn my attention. Since I am bored with my life, I will play for a while, my sweet."

Bored in his life? Why, that condescending arse. He was the bore in life. His pursuit of her friend was boring? Sheffield should be so lucky that Sidney even gifted him a minute of her attention. Lost in her silent tirade toward him Sophia was unaware he had moved close to her once more. He now stood behind her. With the sweep of his hand he brought her hair around to drape over one shoulder. The next thing Sophia felt was the touch of his lips. Slow kisses that he dragged along her neck up to her ear, where he whispered the most scandalous of suggestions. Sophia's knees sagged and Sheffield drew her against his body. His kisses and touch were shocking enough without him saying how he wanted to make love to her. No, what he suggested was not love-making. They were the naughtiest of thoughts that a gentleman should never whisper to a lady. However, he didn't know she was a proper lady of the ton, but rather a lady of the evening.

She tasted like the sweetest spice. He wanted more. When his whispered words caused her to melt against him, he couldn't stop. His hand guided her head to the side as his lips took hers. Ahh, yes. So sweet. He coaxed her lips open with his tongue. As he slid inside, it was to teach her how to kiss. The game of innocence enticed him more. Soon, the girl's experience revealed itself and their tongues meshed in a dance of pleasure. Each stroke only became stronger. He turned her around in his arms, Alex's hands diving into her hair as he consumed her mouth. She was divine. He caught her gasps in between his breaths, each turning longer and into moans of desire.

Sophia was sinking into the pleasures of sin. How one man could spew such arrogance and kiss as a god confused her. She didn't want to stop this madness; it was a pleasure never known before. Her lips followed his. When he stroked inside her mouth, Sophia copied his lead and moved her tongue along with his. His moans and the hold on her conveyed his need. When his hands slid inside her chemise, Sophia could only enjoy the thrill. Before she was aware of his intentions, he lifted and carried Sophia to the divan. She didn't stop him. Not from fear of him learning her identity, but answering to the desire growing inside her.

She wanted more of his caresses. More of his kisses. She wrapped her arms around his neck, pulling his head closer, and ran her fingers through his short, dark tresses. He was the ever-proper duke. But when he kissed her, he turned into the man of her dreams. She'd often read stories about the hero sweeping the heroine off her feet. But no book ever prepared Sophia for the emotions Sheffield stirred in her core.

Sheffield laid the temptress on the sofa and knelt on the floor. The furniture wasn't wide enough to fit both of them comfortably. He only wanted to play. The first time he made love to her, it would be in a bed, not on a couch where anybody could walk in on them. But it didn't mean he couldn't pleasure her for a while. Belle was occupied with another matter. He had time to tempt this sweet girl into becoming his mistress.

As he pulled away, her eyelids fluttered open to reveal the dark amethysts full of desire. He continued to watch her, pulling the buttons of her dress undone to fully reveal her breasts. If he thought her eyes couldn't darken even more, he was wrong. When he spread the chemise wider, his hands slid over her breasts taking one into his palm. When his fingers brushed across her nipple, her eyes grew wide and a moan escaped her. He looked down at his hand and saw the beautiful globe begging to be kissed. When he drew it between his lips and softly sucked, his cock hardened. Aching to be relieved. If he thought her lips tasted sweet, it was nothing compared to her delicious nipples. When her fingers slid through his hair, she guided him to her other breast. This was a woman who understood how her body needed to be pleasured. He drew the sweet bud into his mouth. She arched against him, filled with the same need.

She must stop this insanity. But she could no more pull from his arms than stop him from kissing her. Sophia's mind was in a whirl and wouldn't let her think, because her body didn't want her to. She *wanted* to spin out of control, if this is what crazy felt like. These senses were like floating on a cloud of pleasure. She wanted more. No, she *craved* more. She was past caring who was eliciting these emotions. Her body silently pleaded for Sheffield to continue, tightly strung and begging for release. There had to be more.

Sheffield sensed her body unraveling. He needed to be the man who flew her over the edge. His hand slid underneath her skirts, tracing the silkiness of her legs to the spot he wanted to pleasure. When his fingers swept across her curls, it was to find her wet for him. He lightly traced over her wetness. When she moaned and pressed herself into his hands, he was certain this girl was no innocent miss. She was a woman who wanted him.

When his fingers guided into her wetness, she melted at his touch. Her moans became long-winded sighs of pleasure. Sliding his fingers inside her deeper, he wanted to come right then. She coated his fingers with her warmth. He desired to push her skirts higher and press his mouth against her charms. He ached to sink his cock into the tight core of her body. She tightened around his fingers, close to release.

He drew her lips onto his as his fingers slid in and out of her. The rhythm increasing with each stroke. Her hips rose in time with his hand. Her sighs grew louder as he brought her near the edge. When she fell apart in his arms, her cries echoed around the room. Not wanting anybody to be summoned by the noise and interrupt them, his mouth devoured the enchantress as her passion exploded.

As her body calmed, Sophia realized she lay wrapped in Sheffield's embrace. What came over her? The greatest pleasure imaginable. Her heart beat in a fast rhythm as his hands caressed her. Never in one place for very long. It was as if he wanted to consume her, but at a slow pace. He touched her as if he regarded Sophia as a special prize to treasure. It made her feel vulnerable and cared for. This whole encounter engulfed her in confusion.

Sheffield placed more soft kisses as his hands continued to explore the temptress in his arms. She was an enigma. One he wanted to understand. His hard cock yearned for release pressing into her hip. Still, he didn't want to take her. This reaction was new to him. He felt a sense of sexual fulfillment just by bringing pleasure. Holding her while the girl regained her senses satisfied him.

He needed to withdraw from the room before Belle arrived. Her rule regarding a new girl didn't mesh with him sampling the merchandise. Belle always chose a specific gentleman to introduce a new girl to this profession. This way the girl would not be drawn toward the more powerful gentlemen of the ton and fool herself into believing it was love. When it was only pleasure. All new girls would be shown to mature men who would use them for sex, not young pups who always thought they were in love with whoever they bedded. Nor with any gentlemen of influence.

He was a duke who held power in his own right. But it was his control in Parliament that made him the most powerful. This creature was the last thing he needed to involve himself with now. She was a big mistake. With his pending betrothal to Lady Sidney Hartridge and the article of interest he was having Lord Hartridge research for him, it left Alex no room for distractions. And this temptation that lay in his arms moaning her pleasure was the biggest distraction there could be. Maybe he could find a way for them to amuse themselves without inducing Belle's wrath? He would explain his intentions and work out a deal to spend time with this beauty.

As innocent as she looked when he touched her, she came alive at the pleasures of the flesh. Each stroke of his finger and tongue had her falling apart in his arms. He smiled to himself as a plan formed in his mind. Perhaps they didn't need to involve Belle. He would sneak time in with her with nobody knowing. In the end he would provide well for her in case someone caught them.

He coaxed her head to rise as he placed a gentle kiss to her lips. While he desired to make passionate love to her, he also wanted to treasure her. She invoked a tenderness in him he had never felt with another soul— an emotion he should share with his intended, but didn't. No, she only provoked his anger most of the time. But his involvement and pursuit of Sidney Hartridge was a game he couldn't lose, not even with the temptation of this intoxicating miss.

Sophia leaned into the gentle kiss. She felt a tenderness from him while he held back from his passion. His gentleness undid her. She should lay in his arms in shame. Instead she stayed in his embrace wanting more, reluctant to rise and put herself back together. She must be a wanton at heart. However, he must have thought differently, for he pulled away and rose to his feet. In embarrassment for clinging to him, she tried to set herself right. Her hands shook as she yanked the ribbons tight on her chemise. His hands clasped over hers.

"Easy, love. I am only pulling away, because if I hold you in my arms one second longer, I will ravish you with not a care on who disturbs us. When I make love to you, I want it to be in private. There will be a lock on the door, with no interruptions."

Sophia blushed at his declaration. She'd thought he was dissatisfied and wanted to untangle from her web. Instead he proclaimed his true intentions.

However, this could never happen again.

Her blush was very becoming. She was a supreme actress to be able to blush so easily and to continue her act. He was charmed by her and didn't call her out on her deception. He would indulge her play, because it amused him. Alex tied her chemise and fastened her dress. When she pressed her hands to her skirts to smooth out her wrinkles, he pulled them into his and brought them to his lips. He brushed his mouth across her knuckles with tenderness. When she lifted her head to gaze into his eyes, the soft violet drew him in with a caring expression.

He reached behind her to undo the ribbon on the mask. He wanted to see her face. More than that, he needed to hear her voice. Even though he'd never heard the sweet melody, he imagined it would sink into his soul, for her moans and gasps had certainly brought him to his knees. To hear her speak his name would be heavenly. However, she stopped him before he undid the knot. Again, she silently shook her head in denial.

Now, Sophia panicked. Her heart stilled in her chest. Her hands settled over his, tugging them away from the strings to her identity. How can she convince him not to uncover her face without speaking? Her only thought was something she read in an erotic novel she discovered at the bookstore. She placed her hand on the placket of his trousers. When she encountered his hardness, she stroked, exploring him. The groan that swished between his lips encouraged her. As her palm enclosed around him and she rubbed, he rested his forehead against her as he fought for control. She felt it slipping when he placed his trembling hands over hers to halt her movement, his grip tightening and pulling her fingers away. Sheffield's breathing quickened as he tried to fight against the pleasure. As much as she wanted to continue, even though it was wrong, it stopped him from discovering her true identity. He forgot about untying the mask.

She was a minx. Her action confirmed she was a practiced temptress. She knew exactly how to entice him. When he lifted his forehead from her, he expected to see a cunning smile of control. Except it was a look of wonder and eagerness to play more. She didn't act conceited like most of the women here, but as one who wanted to experiment. He needed to leave. He was in over his head.

Alex walked over to the liquor cabinet to pour himself a drink. He didn't stop at one but drank three shots of Belle's strongest whiskey. The effect of this woman would undo him and soon he would profess his undying love to her. No, it was time he regained control and explained his plans for them. When he turned, he found her gazing into the fire, lost in her own thoughts.

It was then that he took full notice of her. Before him stood a young miss who must have been shunned by her family to be taking up residence at Belle's. Her clothes were from the current fashion plates, and the material itself cost a fortune. It would explain why she held the look of innocence. She must have been tempted, then rejected by a suitor. There could be no other explanation for her sweet behavior and her temptress actions.

During their time together, he would secure her back into the finest grandeur. While he'd made the promise to avoid Belle's and a mistress while he courted Lady Sidney Hartridge, this woman changed his mind. Alex only called upon Belle today to inquire about her troubles, he had no intention of enjoying any pleasures of the flesh. However, this girl tempted him to change his mind. He would enjoy her company. When he was finished with her, he would set her up in a cottage in a faraway village. Far enough away where no word of their relationship found their way into the gossip circle. She would never have to worry about another meal or home in her life, all in exchange for a few months spent in his companionship. Any woman of her status would jump in envy for this arrangement. He wouldn't spoil their time together with the details.

He watched as she twisted her hands nervously. Alex wanted to put her at ease, so he drew her into his arms. Resting his chin on the top of her head, he held her until she relaxed.

"I must leave, my dear. I seek your silence of our time together. Not for me, but for your own good. If Belle were to find I sampled your sweets before the gentleman she assigns you, she will cast you back on the street. I do not wish that for you. Promise me, not a word."

He watched as she nodded her promise to him. With a kiss upon her lips, he stepped back from the temptation of her sweetness.

"I don't know how, but I will find time for us to be together. To discover the passion we are meant to share. Until then, goodbye, my sweet. You will never be far from my dreams."

With that, Sheffield walked away from Sophia. He hesitated at the door as if he was contemplating turning around. Then he strolled out of the parlor as if their time spent together never happened. As Sophia listened to the clock chime, her actions finally sunk into her mind. Not only her mind, but her heart. In their short time together, Alexander Langley, the Duke of

Sheffield, invaded her soul and cracked her shell of anger toward him. If it was possible, she almost believed she fell in love with him. An emotion she dare not explore. He was practically promised to her best friend. Not only that, he didn't know her true identity. He thought Sophia to be a whore meant to pleasure the gentlemen of the ton.

Sophia collapsed on the divan. The very spot where he enticed her to the passion they could share. Her embarrassment changed into remembering the delights of his fingers playing music to her soul. Why? That was all she kept asking herself. Why him? Why her?

Belle rushed into the parlor. Sophia rose from the sofa, expecting a scandal to be lurking behind the Madame. However, it was with instructions from Belle to enclose herself in a cloak. Two of her men would escort Sophia to the carriage waiting in the alleyway.

As Sophia walked to the back door, she glanced around the hallways anticipating Sheffield to show his face. However, they were empty. Nobody stopped them in their tracks. Sophia settled in the carriage, waiting for Sidney to join her.

Sophia was staring out the window, lost in her thoughts, when her friend arrived and sat across from her. The coach swiftly carried them away from their moments in sin. Too absorbed in her own memories, Sophia neglected to take in the appearance of her friend. Sidney held the same look of sexual awakening Sophia did. The emotions Sheffield awakened in Sophia troubled her. She was overcome with sadness, because no matter how he made her feel, they would never be allowed to explore their desires.

~~~~~~~

Alex tried to catch a glimpse of his beauty as Belle ushered her from the parlor, but Belle's men stopped him from interfering. He would have to wait. He was a patient man and she would be worth it. Lingering in the darkened alcove, he watched Belle knock on the door leading to her private chambers. When the door opened slightly, he stared as Belled argued with a gentleman. This new development intrigued Sheffield. Belle never allowed any man into her bedroom.

The mystery was solved as the lady he pursued this season left the room and was rushed out the back door.

Lady Sidney Hartridge held the glow of a woman well pleasured. With her hair in disarray around her shoulders, her clothes wrinkled beyond repair, and her lips full and pouty from being ravaged. Alex's eyes narrowed in anger, for he knew who would soon depart behind her. He wasn't mistaken, Noah Wildeburg strode from the bedroom as a man who'd had his sexual appetite appeased. The devil had bedded the lady Alex set to make his duchess.

It may appear that Alex had lost the game, but he still held one card he could play to win. Wilde would screw it up, he always did. And when he failed this time, Sheffield would be waiting. It would seem he would get his cake and eat it too.

Chapter One

Sheffield cornered Sophia against the tree tucked in the dark recesses of the garden.

"Well, I suppose you will do."

"Do for what?"

"The kiss I was promised."

"I have not promised you a kiss."

"No, you did not. However, your friend lured me into the garden to compromise her. Since she has broken our engagement to trifle with Wildeburg, I have been left abandoned. Therefore, because a kiss was promised, somebody must fulfill the bargain. So, that leaves you."

"You are absurd, no gentleman would suggest such an offer was made."

"I'm not feeling very gentlemanly at the moment, since Lady Sidney passed me over for a mere marquess. As her best friend, Sophia, it falls on to you to console me."

They were hidden in the shadows. Sophia tried to sneak around him, but his body surrounded hers. His hands rested on the tree against her sides, trapping her between the rough bark and his hard body. She gasped as he bent his head to press his mouth to hers. They were warm as they coaxed her lips apart. When his tongue slipped inside, she tasted the whiskey on his breath. As his tongue stroked hers, Sophia felt herself softening into him.

Without realizing her actions, she wrapped her arms around his neck drawing him in closer to their kiss. She heard his moan vibrate off her lips as Alex pulled her away from the tree and enclosed her into his arms.

He only meant to scare her. But his bruised ego fought against the moral code of a gentleman and he'd threatened her with a kiss. If it were not for her interfering, he would still be engaged to Sidney Hartridge. Instead he was once again in the market for a bride. He knew Lady Sophia Turlington aided Wildeburg with winning the affections of Lady Sidney. For that he decided to make Sophia pay. A kiss would warn her against trifling with his life.

How was he to know she could kiss like a skilled courtesan? Her lips should be illegal. He caught her gasps in between his moans. Each stroke of his tongue against hers lighted a fire inside his body for more. He needed to pull back. Since he only meant to frighten her, he didn't want it to go any further, or be burdened with her for a wife. It would appear his search would need to begin again. With a reluctance he couldn't explain he separated himself from her.

As Sophia stood there wild-eyed and gasping for air, he noted her hair had fallen around her shoulders. She presented quite a picture. If she were any other woman and not a vindictive shrew, he would finish what he started. It was a pleasant evening for a tryst in the garden. But Lady Sophia didn't meet his requirements for a duchess. Then there was her mother. He shuddered as he imagined his life married to this lady with her fire-breathing dragon of a mother always present. No, thank you.

He stood before her, raking his eyes over her appearance. With the look of displeasure upon his face, he must have concluded that she didn't stand up to par. Sophia's hair tumbled around her shoulders and she knew her dress was wrinkled from being wrapped in his embrace. However, her dignity was still intact. She lifted her head with pride and raised her chin.

Where in return he cocked his eyebrow in disapproval and smirked at her. Then had the audacity to turn and saunter away, but not before he drawled a snide remark.

"Not what I expected, but it will do."

Sophia stood watching as he walked into the darkness. She pressed her hands to her cheeks and felt the warmth of her blush. She took a few steps backward deeper in the shadows. Her thoughts were a jumbled mess. As her temper rose, she couldn't decide when her anger toward Sheffield turned to being angry with herself. How easy she fell into his arms. Did she not learn anything from their earlier encounter? Her hands fluttered to pull her hair into place. When he ran his hands through her tresses, he'd scattered her hair pins across the lawn. How long were they locked in their passionate embrace? It seemed a few moments, but Sophia knew it to be longer than either of them suspected. Her mother would be searching for her. She must finish repairing herself before she returned to the ballroom. Her palms kept smoothing the wrinkles in her dress over and over as her mind replayed the kiss. How an earth was she attracted to such an irritating, over-bearing ass? What made this even worse was that Alexander Langley had no idea the woman he kissed this evening was the same lady he seduced last week at Madame Bellerose's establishment.

She wandered out of the shadows with her head bent deep in thought, and she ran into somebody. Sophia stood still, afraid of who would regard her in such a mess. She could very well be ruined tonight, with no gentleman to claim her hand in acceptance. Oh, she was no fool to think that the Duke of Sheffield would step up and honor her with a marriage proposal for stealing a kiss. No, he would be an arrogant fool and abandon her to the disapproving ton.

Sophia's body sagged in relief as she looked up to see Lord Roderick Beckwith's concerned face.

"Phee, who did this to you?"

She shook her head, refusing to give him the name of the man who kissed her so thoroughly. Not only thoroughly, but with her fervent response.

"Tell me."

"No Rory, I am fine. Just a little mishap. I stumbled over a root and fell into a tree. As I regained my balance, my dress caught on a piece of bark. Then before I knew it, my hair tumbled down. I cannot find a single pin in this darkness." Sophia rambled on hoping that she distracted him enough so that he no longer looked at her with suspicion.

"Mmm," he responded, searching the ground around them.

"Would you be a dear and send word to Mama about my accident?"

"Yes, but let me escort you to my carriage. It should have returned by now. I promised Sidney I would come look for you."

"Oh, what a mess this evening has become. First Sidney's engagement to Sheffield has broken off. Then Wildeburg spilled her plans for her secret experiment. You are not cross with her, are you? I realize she deceived your friendship, but it was for love, Rory."

"I understand her actions. While I do not approve of them, I do stand by her need for justice. Especially since it concerns Sheffield and Wildeburg. Two men who deserve her wrath. It will be a pleasure to read her thesis in the London Times."

Sophia remained quiet. Rory plainly wasn't aware of Sidney's love for Wildeburg. Sidney herself didn't fully understand her own emotions. Sophia had avoided Sidney all week because of her shame. Tomorrow morning would be soon enough to repair their friendship. She needed to guide Sidney into opening her heart to love. There was nothing she could do tonight.

Rory was able to escort her out of the garden and into his carriage without encountering a soul. After a good night's rest, she would help Sidney achieve her quest for love. When Sidney was settled, she would have to find a way to forget the duke's kisses.

~~~~~~

Sophia arrived at Sidney's the next morning to find her friend in deep thought at her desk. She had parchment strewn all across the room. One finished piece of paper sat before Sidney as she stared at the words. Phee wandered to her side, kneeling on the floor.

"Sid?"

"I love him."

"I know you do, honey, and I am pretty sure he loves you too."

Sidney sighed, "I know."

"He is waiting below in the garden for you. Your mother would like for you to come below."

"No, I must have your help."

"Anything, what can I do for you?"

"First, I want to apologize for being so caught up in my experiment that I have ignored your troubles. Please confide in me, Phee."

"There is nothing to tell. I think it was the sense of loss I felt as I watched you fall in love with Wildeburg. I feared our friendship had reached an end."

The lie slipped so easily from Sophia's lips. The last thing she wanted Sidney to discover was of her two encounters with Sheffield. Sidney needed to focus on her own problems, not to be drawn into Sophia's mistakes. Because mistakes they were. Mistakes that must stop. As long as she avoided Sheffield, then there would be no more secret trysts. No more kisses. No more gasps and moans as he stroked her to life. No more passion.

Passion was an emotion that tempted her into dangerous liaisons with dukes who could ruin her.

"What nonsense, Sophia Turlington. Our friendship will never falter no matter who comes into our lives."

Sidney wrapped Phee into a hug as they laughed at her friend's silliness. Phee knew the dynamic of their friendship would change. Their bond wouldn't be broken, but now Sidney's life would include a husband. Which would leave Phee sharing less time with her friend.

"What are your plans?"

"First, I need you to distract Mama so that I can make an escape. Then you can deliver this note to Wilde and persuade him to return home."

"Where are you escaping to?"

"I need to sneak into Wilde's home. I also need your assistance with that too."

"Leave your mama to me. I have a juicy bit of gossip that will send her out the door to discover if there is any truth to what I have spoken. Then we will spirit you off to your ruination. I told you this would be trouble from the start."

Sidney laughed. "That you did."

Sophia descended the stairs, going in search of Lady Hartridge. She found her in the parlor peering between the curtains and into the garden. She kept sighing as she regarded the man on the bench.

"Isn't it so romantic of him to wait for her?" Sophia whispered over Lady Hartridge's shoulder as she also stared out the window.

"Oh, it is. But it is also such a scandal. Our Sidney is ruined and so is the family name."

"Nonsense. Lord Wildeburg will make right by Sidney. Then the ton will gossip about their love match for years to come.

"Do you think so?"

"Yes. Now Mama wanted me to deliver a message to you regarding Lady Pembroke. She is rumored to be dipping into the Ladies of Mayfair's Homeless Children's funds. It appears she lost at cards and owes a huge sum to Lord Holdenburg."

"Why that … I *knew* she couldn't be trusted to hold on to the mission's funds. I will go to her house right now to collect what money she hasn't gambled away. She will rue the day she used the orphanage's charity for her own sins."

Sophia smiled as she watched Lady Hartridge rant about the devious sins of the loose ladies of the ton. How gambling ruined even the most Christian of women. This part of her plan worked. Now on to step two. Once Sidney's mother rushed from the room and ordered the footmen to ready the carriage, Sophia stepped into the hall and waved to Sidney that the coast was clear. Sidney flew down the stairs and into Sophia's waiting carriage. She then went outside to deliver the note hidden in the folds of her dress to the gentleman waiting in the garden.

When she came upon him, it was to see the once cocky gentleman who'd charmed the skirts off most women sitting dejected on the bench. She settled next to him, holding out Sidney's letter. He took the note and started to unfold it. Sophia rested her hands on his, stopping him. For their plan to succeed, she needed to convince him to return home immediately. They would follow discreetly in her carriage, since neither one of them knew where exactly he resided.

"Wilde, it would be in your best interest to leave. Sidney has written you an explanation. She would like you to return to your townhome to read it. She has explained the reasons for her actions and hopes that you will let the rumors settle before returning. Her greatest fear is that her father will call you out in a duel. Sidney doesn't wish for either of you to come to harm over her obvious mistakes."

"If that is what she wishes. I am only here at her command." He rose from the bench and offered his hand for Sophia to rise.

"Cheer up, Wilde, not all is lost."

Wilde attempted to smile at his new friend, but his heart wasn't into the light banter they usually exchanged. He'd sat throughout the night in the rain for any sign of Sidney's forgiveness. But none came. He continued to wait on the bench through the morning, but still nothing. Now Sidney had sent her friend to get rid of his presence. He had ruined any chance at winning Sidney's love. At that moment exhaustion took hold. He would take Sophia's advice and return home. After a few hours of rest and a change of clothes he would return again to wait for Sidney.

"I will take your word on that, my lady." He pressed a kiss upon her knuckles as he escorted Sophia to her carriage.

Sophia waited for Wilde to walk out of sight before she motioned for her footman to come closer. She directed him to inform the carriage driver to follow Lord Wildeburg at a discreet distance. Soon they were off at a slow pace as they moved through the streets of Mayfair. Sophia sat across from Sidney, watching the excitement fill her eyes as they made their way closer to their destination. Sophia held no envy, but a sense of delight that her serious friend finally opened her heart to the giddy feeling of love. For a while Sophia was unsure if Sidney could even feel the emotion. She was usually caught up in the scientific affairs of her father. Always debating the gentlemen of the ton on issues no lady should be privy to. However, Sidney was unlike any lady Sophia had ever known and she was proud to call her a friend.

Soon the carriage came to a complete halt. Sophia peeked out from the curtains to watch Wildeburg stride into an elaborate townhome. Her mouth opened in shock as she looked upon the grand home. Even as wealthy as her parents were, they owned nothing as magnificent as this. She was joined at the window by Sidney, who gasped as she took in the house she was soon to invade. Sophia rapped on the roof of the carriage and directed them to drive around to the alley behind the house.

When they reached the back of Wilde's home, Sidney started to laugh. Before her in the garden was a trellis reaching upward to an enormous balcony. On the balcony rested a small table with a couple of chairs. It had to be his room. She grabbed a sack on the seat next to her. It was a surprise to lure Wilde into her arms. Sidney grabbed Phee's hands and gave them a gentle squeeze.

"Thank you, and I owe you."

Phee laughed. "Yes, and a big one at that. Now go get your heart's desire, Sidney Hartridge."

Sophia watched Sidney run across the garden and climb the trellis. When she reached the top and swung over the railing, Sidney turned to wave. Sophia returned it and ordered the driver to return her home. The gentle sway of the ride lulled her into a recurring daydream. The same dream that invaded her sleep throughout the nights over and over. With Sophia being pulled into his arms and kissed tenderly with a passion only they shared. Sophia touched her lips as if she could still feel Sheffield's upon hers. Kissing. Tasting. Exploring. Only it was no daydream, but a nightmare she needed to forget. If she kept musing over these emotions, they would only lead her to heartache.

Chapter Two

Alexander Langley was once again a free man. He decided after his kiss in the garden with Lady Sophia that he needed to seek some female companionship. Not the gentile kind, but more of the naughty variety. The type where you can lose your self-control on a woman who would reciprocate with the most unladylike behavior possible. The manner of women he could only find at Belle's. He figured he would sow a few wild oats before he began his search again for the next Duchess of Sheffield. Plus, considering how Lady Sidney Hartridge threw him over for Wildeburg, he deserved a treat. A treat in the sense of long legs wrapped around him throughout the night and into the morning.

He smiled to himself as he strode through the door of Belle's. Ned met him in the hallway informing him that Belle wished for a few words before he enjoyed the delights of her beauties. Yes, maybe more than one tonight would quench his appetite. He wanted to speak to Belle anyway and entice her to share the name of her newest addition. The lady with the violet eyes haunted his dreams with her innocence. However, he knew her innocence to be a game. She kissed as a woman well-versed in the game of desire. Not only her kisses set his mind wandering, but the feel of her soft skin under his fingertips. He'd watched as her body came alive at his touch, and how her gaze changed into a dark amethyst as her passion rose higher. There was much he wished to teach her.

When he arrived at Belle's parlor, it was to find her standing in the doorway, tapping her foot at him in impatience. Belle was a beauty in her own right. With her wild red hair tumbling around her shoulders in waves and the midnight-blue dress hugging her frame, any thought of another woman should vanish from his mind. But their relationship was only one of friendship and nothing more. Not that he wouldn't care to spend a few hours between her bed sheets. He just didn't want to ruin their ties. There was no other woman he respected more than Belle. Their bond went back years, to a time when he was a young lad inexperienced with women. She taught him everything he knew to please a woman, and also how to respect her girls.

"What did I do to deserve your glare?"

"Do not think I don't hear the gossip of the ton. Your actions toward those ladies last night were deplorable."

"They deserved every bit of it, Belle," he said, pushing past her into the parlor.

"Humph, no lady deserves to be treated in that manner, Alexander Langley."

Belle regarded Sheffield as he made his way to her divan, where he spread out in leisure. The man was as arrogant as they came. The right woman needed to put him in his proper place. She wandered to her liquor cabinet and poured both of them a drink. A whiskey for him, and for her a sweet white wine. She needed all the sweetness she could get, if she was to endure the Duke of Sheffield this evening. She was still livid that he ignored her pleas a week ago. At least Wildeburg was enough of a friend to answer her call. If not for him, she didn't know how her girls would have fared with that maniac Lord Dunbarth loose in her home. Belle handed Sheffield his glass. He took it from her hand and tossed back the liquor.

"They do, if they are Sidney Hartridge and Sophia Turlington."

"Wilde is in love with Lady Sidney."

"Pshh. Love is a wasted emotion. Marriages are arranged for the success of generations to come."

"Sheffield, for shame. Love flows between the sheets in my rooms nightly."

"We both know that is not love flowing, but pure lust."

"Perhaps, but is it so wrong to imagine it might be love? Do not tell me, you have never been with a woman and felt an attraction you cannot explain."

Sheffield didn't argue with Belle. For what she spoke held an ounce of truth in the memory of his violet-eyed temptress. Who was she? If he asked Belle, she would deny him the pleasure of her company. But if he didn't argue, Belle would suspect.

"Cannot say I have, sweet Belle."

"One day you will and then all of your arrogant attitude will wither in the wind. Then you will be left humbling yourself for her love. Be warned, my friend, there is a lady who will bring you to your knees."

"Only for me to pleasure her and nothing more."

Belle shook her head at his scandalous comment, realizing she'd pushed the emotion of love with him too far. When he spewed shocking words, it was to cover his emotionless soul. However, Belle was well aware of his caring attitude. If not for his unselfish regard toward herself, she wouldn't be where she was today. He'd picked her up at her lowest and guided her toward a life that satisfied her. That was why, when he didn't respond to her call for help, she became upset and held disappointment for the man he had become.

"You have disappointed me. I have decided to suspend your membership for a short spell."

"No," he roared, coming off the divan.

Surprise crossed Belle's face at his defiance. Something wasn't right with Sheffield, and it had more to do than losing the hand of Lady Sidney Hartridge. As his friend, it was up to her to discover and help ease his troubles. It was what *her* lost love would have wanted.

"Sit, Sheffield," she ordered.

Sheffield returned to the divan and settled into the cushions. Belle rose to refill his glass, bringing the bottle back with her. She had a feeling one would not be enough. As she looked into his eyes, she noticed a trouble she had never seen before.

"Explain."

Alex ran his fingers through his hair in frustration. His life was falling apart before him. All that he had built and achieved would crumble as soon as someone revealed his secret. If he didn't take a bride quickly, and one of a prominent stature, then he would become the laughingstock of the ton. Everybody who envied and admired him would slam the door in his face. He was a farce. He hoped Violet could help him forget his troubles for a while—that was the name he bestowed upon her. Now Belle was barring him from her home. With a hold on his membership, he couldn't find his beauty.

"My life is falling apart," he confided in Belle.

"Because Lady Sidney passed you over for Wilde?"

"No, something more important than that."

"But she was a simple miss. You could have any lady you desire."

"Yes, but her father holds clout with Prinny himself. Their strong relationship would have helped me when my secret was revealed. I had hoped to secure this with my marriage to her."

"What secret?"

"A document was sent to me that refute my family's holdings. If this finding holds truth, it could lay claims of my family's involvement in an assassination attempt on King Henry VIII in the year 1540. This will destroy us."

"Where did you find this?"

"Lord T. is blackmailing me."

"Where is the document now?"

"Lord Hartridge is examining its authenticity."

"Lady Sidney's father? With her involvement with Wilde, would he betray your confidence?"

"No. He is a trusted peer. While he says the detail looks authentic, he is researching its truth."

"Then?"

"I do not know."

"I am sorry, Sheffield. However, it does not change my mind. Your behavior is out of control. You know I do not condone this conduct."

"You are correct, Belle. Please accept my forgiveness for betraying our friendship. I was shallow not to have helped when you called. It was the damn game with Wilde, and in the end he bested me."

"Lady Sidney is an extraordinary woman."

"Yes, she is at that. If I promise to make amends to her, will you allow me access to your girls?"

"You also have to extend your apologies to Lady Sophia too."

"Whatever for?"

"For a certain kiss in a garden you took without her permission."

"How do …"

"I know everything, Sheffield."

"How? There are no rumors spreading about the kiss. If so, her parents would have shackled me to the shrew."

"Another thing you have me to thank for. I tempered the rumor with promises that I must now fulfill, all because of your quick temper growing out of control. How can I help calm you?"

Sheffield sighed at the depths to which Belle intervened in her attempts to keep him from the shun of the ton's eye. He must confess to her of his time with Violet and beg for exclusive rights with the temptress.

"You can let me have the charms of Violet to myself."

"Violet? I have no girl named Violet working for me."

Sheffield laughed. "That is the name I have chosen for her. She would not tell me her name. She had the most remarkable violet eyes I have ever seen."

"Continue to explain yourself. I am at a loss."

"A small confession I need to make, my dear."

"I am listening."

"Last week, when Wilde was in your private bedchamber making love to my intended, I was enjoying the pleasures held in this room."

"I am still confused. With whom?"

"Not going to deny my first statement?"

"No, I am not. You know what happened and used it to your advantage for a while. A gentleman reduced to blackmail does not a good bridegroom make. You deserved to have been thrown over. I will admit that is not what I intended to happen when I called Wilde to my home. She arrived and spoke his name. I thought he could draw her away before any outrage erupted. Instead, he caused a scandal by seducing her in my bedchamber. At least the conclusion of the ordeal led to him finding true love, and all is well."

"Humph …"

"Now, whose pleasure were you enjoying? None of my girls worked that day. We were closed for business due to Lord Dunbarth."

"She was a new girl. A skilled actress who portrayed an innocent, but kissed like a temptress. I am enamored. I will admit to tasting her charms before you could skill her in the rules of your house. Do not blame her, but me. However, I am willing to make you a tempting offer to have her charms exclusively for the duration until I tire of her. Then I will secure her away in the country. I can tell she comes from a family of money and I don't want our names attached to one another. Especially with the drama about to enfold. I don't need an angry papa chasing me down. Since she works here, I assume her family has already disowned her. I will compensate you both very nicely."

"How intimate were you with, 'Violet'?"

"Mmm, enough." Sheffield wouldn't go into further detail. They were between him and his violet-eyed beauty.

Belle tried to keep the look of shock off her face. It took every ounce of her professionalism to not rant at him at the mistake he'd made that day. In her worry over Wilde's actions with Lady Sidney, and the debacle of the previous evening, she had forgotten about the friend. She'd left Lady Sophia Turlington alone in her parlor with a mask to hide her identity when trouble between a couple of girls drew her away upstairs. Now she'd found out that Sheffield tasted her charms.

Oh, this was more trouble than Belle could even have imagined. How would she avoid the scandal, if news of this leaked? This was bigger than any disaster there could be. She needed to think this through to her advantage. How could she prevent Sheffield from discovering the identity of the violet-eyed miss? Belle was aware of the sexual prowess of Sheffield. Her girls bragged plenty when they spent a night in his arms. As an unselfish lover, he satisfied the women as well as they satisfied him.

He'd ruined the girl and it was all her fault. Belle didn't lure Lady Sophia here. But neither did she protect Sophia's virtue.

As she watched Sheffield, her eyes narrowed as she contemplated what he offered. It would appear Lady Sophia nestled under his arrogance and opened him to a need he couldn't explain. She couldn't promise him the lady, because the lady would probably never appear here again. So how could she push Sheffield into the arms of Lady Sophia without either of them being the wiser? She wondered if the miss was as awakened to the same passion as Sheffield. The very lady he called a shrew was the one he wanted to sample more charms from. She smiled at him.

"Your offer is tempting, but I must speak to Violet to see if she would be acceptable to such an arrangement."

"Call her down."

Belle laughed at his eagerness. Sheffield was going to fall and fall hard. Lady Sophia Turlington was just the lady to bring him to his knees.

"I cannot."

"Why not?"

"Because she is not in residence at the moment."

"Where is she?"

"She will return soon. I will send her your offer and let you know her response."

Sheffield sat in frustration. His need for Violet was turning him into a lunatic and Belle was laughing at his expense. Damn her.

"When?"

"When what?"

"When will she return?"

"Soon, Sheffield. You must display a bit of patience."

"You have two weeks to get an answer for me. If not, I will look elsewhere for my needs."

"Very well. Now for me to entice Violet to your bed, you must in return do a favor."

Sheffield nodded. "Anything."

"You will make a sincere apology to Lady Sophia."

"No."

"Sheffield, does not the temptation of Violet in your bed allow you to bend your conceited behavior?"

Sheffield fumed. Belle placed him in a tight spot. She was well aware a duke apologizing to anybody was unheard of. Now, she wanted him to give an apology to a shrew who helped to destroy his laid-out plans. The lure of violet eyes darkening to amethyst, creamy skin begging to be caressed and kisses which turned him to a slave, convinced him.

He sighed as he agreed to Belle's request. "Only for you."

"Excellent."

Belle smiled secretly at her enjoyment of watching the beginning of his fall. How to arrange for them to meet was a problem for tomorrow.

"Sophia may well be your next duchess. You are in need to place yourself in a good standing with a prominent family. What family could be more prominent in the ton than the Turlingtons? While her father is only an earl, he holds much power among the peers of the realm."

"I told you, the girl is a harpy which she has learned at the hands of her mother. Do you think I want to be saddled with those women for the rest of my life? The chaos it would cause with Grandmother. She is enough of a tyrant herself. Have some mercy on me, Belle."

Her laughter lighted the room, calming the anger in her soul. While she was furious with Sheffield for his poor behavior, he was still Alex to her. A young gentleman who picked her up when she was down and held her hand through the battles of life.

She slid over on the couch and laid her head on his shoulder. As his hands wrapped around her shoulders, he teased the locks of her hair with his fingers. They rested silent in their thoughts and in the comfort of friendship. After a while, Sheffield placed a kiss on her head and rose.

"Thank you, Belle."

"You are welcome. I will send notice to you shortly."

Sheffield nodded in approval. While he'd visited Belle's tonight for release from being passed over, he decided it was not what he truly desired. With thoughts of Violet he walked out of the townhome and entered his carriage.

Chapter Three

Sophia stood next to Sidney as she delivered her vows of devotion to Wildeburg. Her experiment ended with her falling in love. Sidney had set out to expose to London the gentlemen of the ton with examples of their unsavory behavior. However, she became involved in her own scandal. Oh, for a scandal to end so promising. The couple was hopelessly in love, and Sophia had helped guide them to this stage in their life.

Her glance slid from them having their first kiss as a married couple to the best man standing next to Wildeburg. Sheffield stood with a frown as he watched the bride and groom, his lips twisting in disapproval. Wilde confused Sophia when he asked Sheffield to stand up with him. Why would any man rejected by the bride be the best man for the groom who stole his fiancée away? Best friend or not, it only drew the throngs to the ceremony. The overcrowded church expected a scene but held disappointment, because all they witnessed was the love of Sidney and Noah.

Sophia's thought changed into more of a sensual nature. As she watched his mouth, all she could imagine was coaxing the frown into a smile. Her tongue tracing his full lips open so she could explore him. Would he taste like whiskey again? She licked her lips as her gaze rose to lock with his. Her eyes widened, but she couldn't look away. His dark stare froze her in place. His eyes narrowed in confusion and he tilted his head in his condescending way, cocking his eyebrow at her glance. She was as bad as

Sidney. Sidney explained how she looked at the gentlemen with the same perusal they did to her. Sophia felt the heat of a blush spreading across her face.

What on earth was she staring at? Sophia Turlington was a strange chit. He pulled his handkerchief out of his pocket and made a swipe across his mouth. Did Grimes leave a spot of shaving cream on his lips? As she continued to stare, he waited for her gaze to meet his. He wanted to give her a look that anybody else would glance away from. But she didn't. When her eyes met his, she continued to stare. He also noticed the blush spreading across her cheeks. Well, at least she was embarrassed that he caught her gawking. When her glance still didn't waver, he shook his head and looked away. It would appear his day would be a long one.

When Wilde approached him with the question to be his best man, Alex had conceded his loss and agreed. He didn't want to lose his friendship with Wilde over a matter of little importance to him. Sidney Hartridge was only a piece to a puzzle in his life. A piece in the end that didn't fit. He was frustrated that Wilde once again had beaten him. Even though he never held a chance to begin with. Now he was saddled with Lady Sophia for the day. Since they stood with Wilde and Sidney at the altar, they were now the honorary guests at the wedding reception. They would be seated together at the bridal table and offer toasts to the happily wedded couple. It was their role to mingle with the other guests. Also, he had that ridiculous apology to make. Belle would hear if he didn't.

Lady Sophia was to ride in his carriage to the reception. There he would offer his apology and agree to a pleasant afternoon for appearance's sake. That should appease Belle enough into making his proposition to Violet.

The church echoed with applause at the married couple. As the pews emptied to proceed to the reception Sheffield offered his arm to Lady

Sophia. He noticed her reluctance as she slid her hand onto his forearm. Her touch was light and not clingy. Most women, when granted his arm, stated their presence by clinging and pressing their body to his side in a most unbearable situation. However, she was a lady personified, with her soft touch and her skirts only brushing across his trousers occasionally as they walked along the aisle. She didn't try to press her breasts to his arm or smother him with perfume. Actually, she smelled sweet. It was a fragrance he couldn't quite recall, and he racked his mind for the memory. He couldn't remember where he caught a whiff of it before. Oh, well it did not matter. For after today, his time spent with Lady Sophia would only be at a minimum. Just because they were both friends with the bride and groom didn't mean they would engage much.

Sophia tried to stay calm as her hand rested on his arm. She wanted to press tighter to feel his strength. However, she resisted. His scent was as intoxicating today as it was on the other occasions she was in his presence. As he escorted her out of the church and handed her into his carriage, she waited for his grandmother to join them. Except he closed the door and tapped on the roof, ordering the driver to take them to the Hartridge's.

"Shouldn't we wait for your grandmother?"

"No, she has joined Lord and Lady Hartridge in their carriage. I wanted a few moments alone with you before the reception."

"This is highly improper. If you escort me into the reception alone, there will be talk," Sophia declared as she settled into the seat.

"There will be no gossip. Nobody would dare to whisper a word regarding my behavior. Also relax, I have no plans to maul you."

"Mmm, your past behavior speaks otherwise. You are a conceited arse, aren't you?"

"Arse? What language coming from a lady such as yourself. But then again, you are no lady are you, Sophia?"

Sophia stilled in suspicion. Did he discover it was her at Madame Belle's?

"What are you implying, Your Grace?"

Sheffield sighed. This wasn't what he'd intended. Instead of apologizing, he'd insulted her. He ran his hand through his hair, frustrated at the position he put himself in.

"Nothing," he mumbled.

Now she was more confused than ever. Did he know? Impossible. If he knew her to be the lady in the mask, he would have exposed her. It was in his nature. Sophia sighed as she relaxed against the carriage cushions. Her secret was safe. For now, anyway. He must be referring to all the times she called him on his rude behavior. She waited for him to speak as she stared out the window. The passing scenery was homes filled with beautiful landscapes. One day, Sophia hoped to have a house of her own where she could make a home with a loving husband. Where their children would run the grounds playing their silly games. Sidney had embarked on that journey today.

Her sigh echoed loudly around the silent carriage. Her glance swept to Sheffield to see he paid no attention to her and was deep in thought. If he only knew that he consumed hers. For the image of the loving husband that kept floating in her mind was of him. Which was preposterous. There was not a loving bone in his body. Sexual yes, but loving, no. Plus, if he discovered Sophia was his mystery lady, the sexual would be replaced with disgust. Her gaze once again returned to the window, because it was a much safer view. She would embarrass herself again if she continued with her fascination of him. He'd already regarded her haughtily when he caught her staring inside the chapel.

"I wanted a private word with you before we reached the reception. It seems I owe you an apology for my past behavior in your company. It was ungentlemanly of me to kiss you in the garden. Lady Sidney injured my pride, and in my frustration I took advantage of your innocence. For that I humble myself for your forgiveness."

Sophia didn't know how to react. She sat dumbfounded until a reply flew out of her mouth.

"The great Duke of Sheffield sinks to bestow someone as lowly as a mere mortal of my standings an apology. Will wonders never cease? I feel the world should shake at such a declaration."

"You're an ungrateful shrew. I knew you wouldn't accept my kind gesture with your own kind acceptance. I don't understand why I bothered."

"Yes, why did you bother, Sheffield?"

"For reasons I would not normally burn your ears with. However, if you must know, I asked a favor from a friend and in return for said favor, I was to apologize to you."

"So, I am only a means to an end."

"Something like that."

"Wait, if your friend knows of our kiss in the garden, then so do other people. You ruined me. I will not be burdened with you for a husband."

"I was not aware I offered."

"Well ..." Sophia stuttered.

"Your virtue is safe and so is your reputation. At least from me, anyway."

"That wasn't the case the evening of the Havelock Ball."

"I already explained my reasons. You were available. Any other woman would have satisfied me. Probably more so," he laughed. "Your innocence hardly has the desired effect on a man such as myself."

Sophia didn't have to reply. The carriage had arrived at its destination and the door opened. Sheffield alighted and reached for her hand. He asked if she accepted his apology and Sophia nodded in agreement as he helped her down the stairs. All she could think of was how misleading he was. Her very innocence enticed him to a passion she wanted to explore.

They entered the Hartridge residence with no regard mentioned to their time alone. Everybody only paid attention to the newly wedded couple. Thoughts of Alexander Langley moved to the back of her mind as she decided to enjoy the day rejoicing in her friend's happiness. She would endure his company when needed, other than that he would have to become a forgotten memory. Their personalities did not mesh, and they never would.

Chapter Four

With Sidney away on her honeymoon, Sophia found too much free time on her hands. It was too quiet. She read all the new novels at the bookstore, even reread her hidden treasures. Something she should have resisted, but she couldn't forget, was the memory of Sheffield's kisses. Thoughts of him consumed her day and night. The nights were the worst. Her passionate dreams would awaken her, and she would lay frustrated that her desires would go unsatisfied. It didn't help that every ball or musical she attended, he was present. Gossip spread among the ton about his search for a bride. Whenever their paths crossed, he offered a courteous acknowledgment. They shared no conversations, no dances, and were never alone. Which only made Sophia yearn for him more. At least, when they were arguing, it gave her a reason to hate him. Since he displayed a polite indifference, it must mean he never thought of her the same way she did him.

As Sophia sat surrounded by a circle of friends, their gossip floating over her head, she noticed him. He was being introduced to Lady Dallis MacPherson. After he secured a dance with the new beauty, he joined a group of gentlemen where he shared a drink as they talked. When the musicians began to play, he approached Lady Dallis to escort her onto the dance floor. Sophia watched as they glided through the set.

As her friends' gossip turned into whispers, she heard Sheffield's name mentioned. Her ears perked to the conversation as her eyes traced their steps. The discussion revealed Sheffield's plans on pursuing Lady Dallis's hand. He wanted her to be his duchess. But there were other rumors floating around with his infatuation of a miss named Violet. Nobody knew Violet's identity, and they were curious as to what kind of beauty drew the duke's attention enough to announce his interest. Whoever this woman was, every available lady in the ton was jealous. Sophia's heart sunk even deeper. Not only was he courting Dallis with a waltz, he was enamored of another beauty. It was hopeless. Sophia rose from her chair. She could no longer watch or listen to whispers of Sheffield. She took her leave and wandered to the balcony.

As she leaned over the railing gazing at the stars, she felt a gentle nudge against her ribs. When she glanced to her side, it was to see her friend Lord Rory Beckwith. He smiled at her, wagging his eyebrows to bring a smile to her face. She gifted him with a small one as she turned back to the stars. Soon one shot across the sky.

"Make a wish," Rory said.

Phee closed her eyes. The wish she made would never come true, but that was what wishes were for. Dreams of the deepest possibilities mixed with magic.

"Well?"

"You are not supposed to utter your wishes, or they won't come true."

"Why so sad, Phee?"

"I am not sad, Rory."

"I know I am not Sidney, but we have been friends long enough for me to realize when you are troubled."

"'Tis nothing."

"Nothing as in, you will not confide in me?"

"Nothing as in I'm not quite sure. I feel lost. Does that make any sense?"

"A little. It's different without Sid, isn't it?"

"Yes, I suppose that must be what it is."

"Shall we take a ride in the park tomorrow? We can even feed the ducks, if you wish."

"I would like that very much, Rory. An outing is just the thing I need."

"Excellent. Now, shall we dance?"

Sophia laughed. She could always count on Rory to pull her out of her doldrums. Next to Sidney he was another great friend. With him she could be herself and never worry. Not only a friend, he was also like a brother to her and Sidney. He protected them and looked out for their safety.

"Yes. Thank you, my lord."

"My pleasure, my lady."

Before they could enter the ballroom Sheffield and Lady Dallis were coming their way. The duke maneuvered the redhead beauty off the dance floor and onto the balcony. Rory tugged Sophia aside and drew her behind a potted plant, hiding them. They stared as Dallis pulled herself out of Sheffield's grasp and slapped him across the face. However, she wasn't finished as she continued with a rather long lecture of his boorish behavior and threatened him with unsavory actions. Her Scottish brogue emphasizing how she would hang him by his bollocks if he ever so much as spoke to her again. Sophia tried not to laugh at the exchange. But the devil in her gave into a fit of giggles revealing their hiding place. She was not the only one, for Rory held onto his side with laughter.

Rory said, "I better rescue the lass, before the crowd inside notices this scene. I will return for our dance shortly."

Phee couldn't stop giggling as she nodded. By now tears flowed from her eyes at her enjoyment.

Rory approached Lady Dallis. "Excuse me. May I escort you to your grandmother, miss?"

She gave him a thin smile. "Mmm, look, a gentleman in London. Observe and learn, Your Grace, on how a gentleman should treat a lady. Yes, you may kind sir."

Rory held in his pleasure as the mere girl handed Sheffield a critique on his manners. He took hold of the young lady's hand and re-entered the ballroom. Sophia was forgotten as Rory became entranced by the beauty's spell. Lady Dallis's voice soaked inside him and made Rory feel as if he had finally come home.

"Oh, your charm knows no bounds, Sheffield." Sophia continued to giggle.

Sheffield's temper hung by a thin thread. To be slapped, yelled, and now giggled at, set him in a fine mood. For two weeks he'd displayed common courtesy toward Sophia Turlington. While avoiding her at social functions, he was able to keep his irritation toward her in check. He even treated her with a polite manner when they came into contact. Now, as she stood before him laughing at his expense, he wanted to hurt her.

Later, after he had a few drinks, he would realize she was not at fault for his foul mood. He was frustrated in the search for the perfect duchess and Belle's avoidance on the subject of Violet. His two-week threat ended this evening. His one chance with Lady Dallis resulted in disaster and there would be no Violet—an infatuation that had become an obsession over those past few weeks. An obsession he needed to part with.

For now, Lady Sophia would pay the price for his temper.

He grabbed and pushed her into the dark shadows. He should have stopped when her giggles turned into a gasp. But her lips tempted him as she licked them. It was more than he could bear.

"I see time has not curbed your tongue any. Let me see if I can help," he whispered.

He hungrily kissed his annoyance on her lips. Instead of fighting him off and yelling to bring attention their way, she opened her mouth beneath his. When she slid her hands around his neck and returned his kiss in full, he forgot any good intentions. His abstinence from sex for the last couple of months aggravated him, and for some unknown reason Sophia Turlington was becoming another distraction. His anger toward her always sent Sheffield to this edge. An edge to jump off and take her with him. What further confused him was how he felt the same connection toward Lady Sophia that he did with Violet. Maybe it was the innocence Sophia held that reminded him of his violet-eyed temptress? They had many similarities, which only fueled his desires.

Finally, he was kissing her. Sophia knew it was wrong and should protest. She thought it would never happen again. She no longer cared if they were caught. Her lips opened under his, begging for more. Their tongues performed a dangerous dance as their passion grew higher. When his hands raised her skirt and brushed across her core, she moaned into his mouth and pressed herself into his hand, whimpering. She needed his touch. Her body ached for anything from him. When his finger slid inside and stroked, her knees buckled. He caught her as he continued the pleasure on her body. He stroked faster as his kiss went beyond frustration to need.

My god, she felt like heaven. His finger found a rhythm inside her wet mound, his thumb flicking across her clit. He captured her moans inside his mouth as he ravaged her lips. Each kiss hungry for more. She was fulfilling a need in him that he didn't realize he craved. When he sent her flying over the edge, Sheffield felt complete. She satisfied his ache for the moment. He knew he needed more, but not with her. While he sampled her delights, he would not trap himself with Lady Sophia. He pulled away from her as she sagged against the brick wall. Her eyes huge as she gasped for air. He lowered her skirt and stepped back. He slid his finger inside his mouth licking off the taste of her, still hungry. Her eyes grew larger, displaying her innocence toward his act. Then he laughed at her.

"Mmm. Yes, I seemed to have silenced you into submission." With those parting words, he strolled away.

Sophia couldn't recall how she made it through the rest of the evening. Somehow, she repaired her dress and hair in the darkness. Then she found her mother and pleaded a headache. As she lay in bed replaying their time in the shadows, she couldn't even begin to understand Sheffield. When he kissed and caressed her, she felt a sense of them as one. But when he spoke, he was a brute. Her feelings were a conflicted mess. The longer she replayed his final words, the more anger took hold. Silenced into submission? We shall see about *that*, Alexander Langley.

Chapter Five

"Now you, my friend, are the distracted one, not I."

"Sorry, Phee," Rory mumbled as his gaze searched among the other riders in the park.

"Are you searching for anybody in particular?"

"Mmm …"

"Rory Beckwith, hasn't your mother ever told you it is bad manners to ignore the lady you are with?" Phee laughed as she teased him.

Sophia stared as a blush spread across Rory's cheeks. Which made her laugh harder. The big brute blushed like a maiden. She couldn't wait to tell Sidney about this, so they could tease him unmercifully. It was not, however, a very becoming shade on him, what with his red hair. It was amusing to watch.

Rory sighed as he remembered he'd brought Phee on the ride to cheer her spirits. Not to ignore her while she felt lonely with Sidney away on her honeymoon. He reined in the horses and stopped them near a tree. His search was over. The lady he sought would have to wait. He needed to be a friend, not a desperate suitor. It didn't matter anyway. The girl he wanted was far out of his league. But he could hope and fool himself with his dreams. He reached to help Phee from the cart. They strolled along the promenade, nodding to their other fellow walkers. He guided her closer to the pond where they sat upon a bench. Reaching into his pocket he pulled out a wrapped package and put it on Phee's lap. She bestowed him with a smile as she unwrapped the paper with glee. Soon a string of ducks waylaid them as they clamored for the bread that Phee tossed onto the grass. Rory relaxed against the bench and enjoyed the scene.

"Hush, you will all get a bite," she scolded the ducklings.

Rory laughed. "I didn't bring that much bread."

Sophia released a tinkling of laughter. "You should have filled both of your pockets."

They watched the ducks finish their treat and waddle back to the pond. Each of them falling into a line between their parents, the mama duck leading them into the water, as the papa duck stood behind to make sure they didn't lose any kids along the way.

"Who is she?"

Rory realized he would have to admit his infatuation, or Sophia would never let up. "Dallis MacPherson."

"Oh, but …"

"Yes, I know."

Rory understood his impossible dilemma. Nobody comprehended it better than he, how desperate his financial standings stood. Also, he was aware of how Dallis's grandfather wouldn't let her marry anybody but a gentleman of wealth. Not only that, but the gentleman must hold one of the highest positions in the realm to further their holdings. And he, Rory Beckwith, was not that man. But the Duke of Sheffield was. However, Lady Dallis had made it more than clear that she wasn't interested in the duke. Maybe by some luck Rory had a chance?

Sophia slipped her arm through Rory's and offered him a hug. She laid her head against his shoulder as they watched the water. It was windy, so little white caps appeared on the surface bouncing up and down as the gusts blew. They were attracted to the wrong people. Sophia to a man who showed her no ounce of respect, and Rory to a woman above his means. They were a sorry sight.

"Perhaps, we should marry, Phee? I like you and you like me. Then we wouldn't have to muster through these silly functions that the ton insists on making a union."

"We would kill each other with kindness on the first day, Rory. I love you too much as a friend to burden you with my mother for a mother-in-law."

Rory cringed, he forgot about her mother. "Ahh, you might have a point." He quickly rescinded the offer.

Sophia laughed. Her mother was the main cause why no gentleman offered for her hand. Every season they would court her, and her mother would always ruin her options. No man wanted Lady Turlington for a mother-in-law. Her mother meant well, but it remained the reason Sophia was on her fourth season. In truth, Sophia used her mother as a buffer, for there had yet to be a gentleman who interested Sophia enough to marry. Yes, they all had money, power, and treated her with respect. Unlike a certain gentleman who consumed her thoughts this season. But she didn't love them. She wanted love when she married. To be loved and cherished forever by the man of her dreams. And none of these gentlemen provided her with that. Maybe she should accept Rory's offer and move on with her life? If she married another man, her need for Sheffield's kisses would surely vanish. Oh, who did she fool? That desire would surface. She was doomed until she removed Sheffield from her thoughts. If only he would stop kissing her. Going forward, she must make sure nobody leaves her alone with him under any circumstances.

Someone covered her eyes. "Guess who?"

Sophia released a sound of glee as she jumped off the bench. She turned to see her friend wearing a smile of contentment. Sidney's new husband stood by her side bestowing her with a smile of amusement. Sophia ran around the bench and enclosed her friend in a hug.

"Sid," Sophia exclaimed.

"Oh, Phee, I missed you so much. I told Noah we had to come find you. Your mother said Rory took you for a ride in the park. I knew you would be feeding the ducks."

"I have missed you too. Rory took pity on me today, but I am afraid we have not raised our spirits any."

Sidney tugged Phee away from the men. She could tell that whatever troubled her friend before she left on her honeymoon still bothered her today. When they were near the trees, she turned Phee to face her and stared at her for a while. Yes, something was weighing on her mind. While Sidney wanted to share her happiness with Phee, she understood it was the wrong time.

"What troubles you?"

"Nothing."

"Nothing my arse, spill it, friend. I know you better than yourself."

"Wow, what language spews out of your mouth now that you are a marchioness."

"Sophia Turlington!"

"Very well. Where do I begin?"

"Usually from the beginning helps."

Sophia started to walk along the bank and Sidney followed her. Sophia stopped and turned around.

"I am only going to say one name and it should explain all. I will not go into further detail, for the moments are private. Those that I wish to keep to myself. I think you understand, since you kept certain details of your intimate relationship with Wilde to yourself."

Sidney wanted to hear more, but Sophia had a point. She did keep a lot of moments shared with Wilde private. Sidney would make a promise now and hope over time she could persuade Sophia into revealing more. She nodded in agreement. She waited for Sophia to mention Rory, because when Wilde and she walked behind them, they seemed to be sharing a special moment. She understood Sophia would be troubled that she was changing the dynamics of her relationship with a friend. However, when Sophia revealed the name of her troubles, the only thing Sidney could do was stand in shock.

"Sheffield." With the one name mentioned Sophia turned from Sid and rushed back to the two gentlemen. Sophia knew if she could reach them before Sid caught her, she would be safe. Sophia stood next to Rory, and Sidney arrived a few moments later glaring at her—*we will talk soon*. They had been friends for so long that the other could interpret each stare, or glare for that matter. A quick shake of Sophia's head refuted the look. Sidney returned the gesture with narrowed eyes and a cock of her head, portraying *we shall see about that*. Sophia knew Sid would be tenacious about learning more. She needed to convince Rory to leave before Sidney withdrew her promise.

"Rory, the hour is growing late. I do not want to worry mother. Would you mind taking me home?"

Rory winced to think of the lecture he was sure to hear from Lady Turlington if he kept Sophia from her other engagements. He also felt relief. Wildeburg was the last chap he wanted to talk with. Rory held anger at the marquess for seducing his friend and involving Sidney's family in a scandal. While he felt happiness for Sidney, he harbored resentment toward her husband.

Rory himself tried to capture Sidney's heart but failed. He was a sore loser.

"Yes, we must bid you goodbye. So glad you are home, Sidney, I shall see you at your parents'."

"Yes, I am eager to return to helping Papa with his research. Is he still working on that secret project?"

"Yes, he is, but he has not confided in me yet."

"Mmm, perhaps we can help each other with that."

"Yes, I believe we might be able to. Some new information has come to light that I think you will find interesting."

"Excellent, please visit me for tea tomorrow and we can discuss the matter."

Sophia watched their exchange, curious about this secret research. Why was Rory so eager to help Sidney now? Lord Hartridge only kept a project private to protect the individual that asked for the research. Rory would always keep Sidney from prying. Now he wanted to help her locate the research and divulge the information. Whose research was it?

Rory was already guiding the horses from the park. She needed to find out from him before he delivered her home.

"May I ask, whom is Lord Hartridge protecting?"

"Sheffield," Rory snarled.

His dislike for the duke was no secret. While before he tolerated Sheffield's presence at the Hartridge's, it turned to hatred when he discovered Sheffield tried blackmailing Sidney into marriage. It all made sense. With Sheffield's interest in Lady Dallis, and Sophia confiding in Sidney the name of her distress, it prompted Rory and Sidney into discovering the duke's secrets. Oh, what a mess. How could Sophia prevent them from uncovering his secret? If Sidney continued down a path to destroy Sheffield, nobody could stop her. Once Sidney's mind was set, the mess usually began. Only this time, Sophia's own secrets involved the duke. If Sophia's involvement with Sheffield were discovered, it would ruin her.

Sophia must ask a favor from her new friend Wilde. Sophia would need his help to distract Sidney from her newest agenda. While Sheffield might deserve whatever Sidney had in plan for him, Sophia must protect herself.

Rory walked Sophia to her door. "I am sorry I was not the best of company for our ride."

"I understand, we are both distracted with our own problems. Can I ask you a small favor, though?"

"Anything for you, my dear."

"Please reconsider helping Sidney find the missing document concerning Sheffield. I would hate for you to lose the trust of Lord Hartridge."

"I am surprised you would protect the duke. Your hatred of him while he courted Sidney was well known. Also, considering his recent actions toward you, it is one of the main reasons I am agreeing to Sidney's plans."

"What actions?"

"The ones where he accosted you in the garden and on the balcony. I am ashamed of myself for not coming to your honor. It was my selfishness that has kept me silent. I cannot afford to have Sheffield ruin me; I must care for my mother and sister."

"You knew?"

"Yes, please forgive me."

"How much did you see?" Sophia turned red in embarrassment, ashamed that Rory knew her secrets.

"I only saw your appearance from both times after he left you, nothing more. I drew my own conclusions. Am I wrong in what I assume?"

Sophia stayed silent. He didn't realize the full scope of her involvement with Sheffield.

He said, "That is what I thought. Your secrets are safe with me. I cannot promise the favor you are asking. This is the only way I can defend your honor. However, you must promise me to never allow yourself to be alone with him. Promise me, Phee."

"Both times would never have happened if my friends had not abandoned me. Do not play me false, Rory Beckwith, with your words on defending my honor. You are only out for Sheffield because of his courtship with Lady Dallis. Jealousy rules your mind at the moment. You are not trying to honor your friend. So, since you cannot promise me, I cannot promise you. Good day."

Sophia stormed into the house, slamming the door behind her.

Sophia continued to her room, furious with her friends. As she walked into her bedroom, she removed her bonnet and gloves, throwing them on the bed. She paced back and forth across the rug, her mind whirling with thoughts on her situation. Her emotions were in a tumble and she needed to sort them out before she moved forward. Usually a very calm person, she felt like a whirlwind blowing here and there. All her emotions needed to be grounded. Her erratic behavior even bothered herself.

A note on her desk caught her eye. Unlike anything she had ever seen before. It was pink vellum with decorative handwriting. When she turned it over, it was stamped with a B. No crest adorned the stamp. As she brought the letter to her face, she smelled the musky perfume from the parchment. The fragrance was heavy. Sophia only had one word to describe it. Sexy. Intrigued, she unfolded the paper.

Lady Sophia,

I understand this would be highly regarded as a scandal for you to receive an invitation from a Madame. However, I am in need of your assistance in a matter of great importance. I am reaching out because when we met, I felt a kindred spirit as I glanced in your eyes. If you would please join me for tea today at three o'clock I would greatly appreciate your generosity. When the hour arrives and you are not present, I will understand. It is only under the duress of scandal falling at your feet. If you come to tea, I will share with you my request. There will be no pressure for you to agree, for I have only promised that I would ask you. However, you choosing to decide on what I will ask will be entirely at your discretion.

Until three o'clock, my lady.

Madame Bellerose

Chapter Six

Sophia held the note to her chest as she took deep breaths trying to slow down her heartbeat. She glanced around the room, expecting her maid to be lurking. When nobody burst through her bedroom door, demanding answers as to why she received a letter from a brothel, Sophia brought the note before her eyes again. She scanned the letter, hoping she could decipher the hidden meaning between the lines. When she was unable to understand why Madame Bellerose requested her presence at tea, her curiosity got the better of her.

On her previous visit to the brothel, the Madame fascinated her. She portrayed herself as a woman of the highest esteem, even though she wasn't. The woman displayed kindness by concealing Sophia's identity from any customers. If she had been compromised, Sophia didn't think Belle would have issued an invitation for tea. No, there must be another reason for the invite. Sheffield? Did he request her? Sophia's heart quickened at the thought. The temptation to be held in his arms prompted her to change her clothing.

She needed to sneak away from her mother.

Sophia changed into a new dress without the help of her maid. She pulled her hair into a simple bun, placing a bonnet with a veil over her face. The hat concealed her identity. As she walked downstairs, she heard no whisper of a sound in the house. When she passed a footman, he handed her a note. She stepped into the parlor to read the message. Her mother ordered her to pack her bags and reside at Lord and Lady Hartridge's for the duration of their absence. They were called away on a matter that required their attention at their estate in the country. They would return within two weeks. Her mother also left a note for Lady Hartridge explaining Sophia's need to stay with them. She didn't have enough time to contact Sidney's parents before they departed and needed Sophia to deliver the note for her.

This couldn't be going any more her way with this bit of news. Not only could she sneak out to Madame Belle's, Sophia could indulge in her love of reading romance novels without her mother badgering Sophia to accompany her to one function after another. The only downfall, it would be harder to avoid Sidney if she stayed at her parent's home. Sophia decided to ignore her mother's directions and stay at home. She knew of the consequences of her actions, but didn't care. The pull of Madame Belle's letter tempted her into throwing caution to the wind.

Sophia directed the footman to call her a hackney. When he suggested the family's carriage, she declined stating charity work as her designated stop. He did her bidding with the understanding that she didn't like to display her wealth to the less fortunate. As she settled in the hackney, the footman declared her need for a chaperone. As he returned to the house to have a maid attend her, Sophia gave directions for the driver to deliver her to Madame Belles' with due haste.

The hackney flew down the road, passing one carriage after another. As they rounded the corner, Sophia swore it was done on two wheels. The vehicle hung on one side longer than the other. She held on to the strap and prayed for her dear life. But not once throughout the wild ride did she doubt her decision to visit the brothel. When they came to a skidding stop outside the alley to Madame Belle's, Sophia offered a small thank you on arriving at her destination in one piece.

The hackney driver released a pelting whistle drawing attention their way. Sophia lowered her head, rushing to the house. The door opened and Ned, Belle's doorman, ushered her inside. Sophia remembered his name from her previous visit. He was a startling man, covered in scars and had a rough exterior. However, it was his kindness to her security that she remembered the most. He sent a scowl to the driver ordering him to leave the property immediately.

"Welcome, my lady. Belle has been expecting you. Please follow me," he urged her in a soft voice. Another strange aspect about the man. His quiet voice didn't match his physical appearance.

"Thank you, Ned."

He turned his head in surprise that she remembered his name. A look of respect lit his eyes before turning and opening the door to Belle's parlor. After Sophia walked into the room, the door closed and Sophia could hear the lock click. Nobody would interrupt her visit. Sophia felt a fresh sense of calm that while she was here, her presence would be protected.

"Lady Sophia, I was hoping my letter did not frighten you away." Belle rose to welcome Sophia into her parlor. When she clasped her hands, she held them, looking deep into Sophia's eyes. Their gazes connected. Yes, they did share a kinship. How weird that you could experience a bond of friendship with somebody you only just met.

"I will admit to no fright, but an extreme sense of curiosity instead."

"Please join me on the sofa, I had cook prepare tea and dessert for our visit. I hope you like lemon squares."

"Actually, they are my favorite."

"Excellent, my cook made an abundance. Another friend who is coming to dinner tonight loves them as well and I have promised him a few. Well, that is if we do not eat them all now. It would serve him right." Belle laughed.

"I would hate to disappoint your friend. However, once one passes between my lips, I admit I cannot stop from devouring them all."

"I heard the wonderful news of your friend Sidney's marriage to Lord Wildeburg. They make an enchanting couple, do they not?" Belle poured their tea.

"Yes, Wilde was the perfect man for her. Hopefully, he can learn to curb her need for everything to be an experiment."

"I'm afraid, from what I have heard, he will only indulge her every wish."

"You are probably correct. I only speak out of fear on becoming her next research project."

"What kind of research?"

"She wishes to find the perfect love match for me. For somebody who always swore romance and love wasn't real, Sidney has suddenly changed her mind due to her own circumstances. I fear nobody will be safe from her interference."

"I envy your friendship with one another. You are very close."

"As close as sisters, if we were so."

"That helps to understand her reason then. She only wants you to find the same happiness she has captured."

"Yes, however at the moment 'tis near impossible."

"May I inquire why?"

"A certain gentleman has put me under his spell. However, he is spiteful except for the moments when he is kissing me. I know I should not speak of this, but I sense you can keep a secret."

"Yes, dear, and I will keep yours."

"That is why I have accepted your offer for tea. I needed somebody to confide in who wouldn't judge me."

Belle offered her the plate of lemon squares. Sophia consumed several as she explained her encounters with Sheffield. Belle didn't judge or interrupt as Sophia tried to explain her feelings for the unbearable man. Before Sophia knew it, she'd eaten the entire offering of the sweet dessert. Also, a weight had been lifted from her shoulders.

"Please extend my apologies to your friend. There are no treats left for him."

Belle smiled as she assured Sophia that her friend would understand.

While Belle sensed Lady Sophia would agree to Sheffield's invitation, she was furious at him for his reprehensible behavior. How dare he accost this lovely creature for his own whim? She deserved better than him. But Belle saw the same connection between this couple that their friends shared. In the end she knew Lady Sophia would bring Sheffield to his knees. Hopefully, in the meantime, Sheffield could curb his arrogance. Belle feared that to lose this lady would be his last chance at redemption. She hated to deceive Lady Sophia, because she felt a friendship forming, but if she could draw these two souls together in love, then it would be worth the deception.

Sophia rose from the divan and wandered around the room. She admired the classic beauty. "Your parlor is lovely."

"Thank you, my dear. I will hold your confidences close to my heart. However, you are excluding the main scene from your interaction with Sheffield, are you not?"

Sophia spun. "I don't understand."

"I think you do. The previous time you visited, you encountered Sheffield. Did you not?"

"How …"

"Nothing passes my attention. Even though, to be honest, your time spent alone with Sheffield did. I apologize for risking your virtue. Between your friend's scandal and my own problems, I was otherwise occupied. I'm unsure on how I can make amends to you."

"There is nothing to make amends on, because nothing happened."

Belle beckoned Sophia to return to the couch and held her hands between hers. "Sheffield calls you 'Violet' and requests your undivided attention. He holds the belief you are my new girl. Your beauty enamored him. Though I imagine it's more than your beauty that grasps his attention. Your time together has sparked a flame inside him."

"But …"

"Yes, I am fully aware of the unorthodox request. How do I inform him the girl he requests is not one of my girls, but a lady of the ton? On the other hand, if you decide to accept his offer, how do we hide your identity? Is this something that would interest you?"

"I do not know if I should be flattered or offended."

"How do you feel?"

Sophia blushed. "Flattered," she whispered.

"You are interested?"

"Yes."

"I thought perhaps you might be."

"How?"

"You are here, having tea in my parlor. If your imagination was not curious about my invitation having to do with Sheffield, why else would I invite you here?"

"My wishful thinking convinced me it could only be because of him."

"Well, you were correct. This situation will be on your terms, my dear. He won't set the rules, you will. Are you sure of your decision? This will ruin your virtue and no gentleman will marry you. You can still walk away and nobody would be the wiser."

"I am aware of my options. However, my heart and the feelings Sheffield arouse within my body are begging me to say yes. I will feel these emotions with no other man but him. If I do not grab this opportunity, then it will be a decision I shall regret for the rest of my life."

"Very well. What are your requirements?"

"I must wear a veil; he can never learn my true identity. He must agree to this. The only problem I have is that during the time we spent together in this room, I did not speak. I will have to, won't I?"

"Yes, my dear."

"He will recognize my voice. How will I be able to fool him?"

"That is easily remedied. You are not aware of your own capabilities. Your voice takes on a huskiness when you speak emotionally, different from when you are angry. Also, take in the factor that while he is in your company as 'Violet' he will not be thinking with his head. He will not pay attention to your voice, only on how you make him feel."

"What about my virginity?"

"I will explain to him how your virtue was never fully ruined. Then, I will discuss with him the terms of your mask and if he wants to take your virginity. If he does not agree, then there is no contract. I will only ask you one more time, before I continue. Are you committed to this arrangement?"

"Yes. However, it can only be for a short while. A week only. After that he must release me and forget about our time together. If he will not agree, then we cannot move on."

A knock sounded against the door. Belle went to answer and whispered with Ned about a problem needing her attention. With directions issued, Belle closed the door and turned. With an observing eye, Belle watched the beauty as she sat calmly on the sofa. She'd underestimated the young lady. She expected Sheffield's offer to offend Lady Sophia. But as they talked, it was obvious Lady Sophia's feelings for Sheffield were about as powerful as Sheffield's were for the young girl. She wished no ill harm to reach her on this arrangement, but Belle knew in her heart that Sophia was the one for Sheffield. The man may not realize he needed a happily ever after, but he did. And Belle would be the one to give it to him.

"Will you be able to stay here for a few hours tonight? It appears Sheffield is here and requesting your answer. He doesn't know that you are here. But I informed him I would have an answer. It would appear he is impatient to know what you have decided. If he approves of your stipulations, he will demand to see you. I can prepare a room for your time together filled with a wardrobe of attire more appropriate for your meeting, and a variety of masks for your approval."

Sophia rose and walked to the window. She stared out at the dusk settling for the evening. The sun was dipping low casting dark shadows in the backdrop. She was confident in her decision, and her need to see him overruled all practical thoughts. While nervous, she also held an excitement to be with him. With a deep breath, she turned to Belle with a nod.

"I will need to write a note to send home."

"Excellent, let me show you to your room, so you can prepare. Do you need me to explain love-making to you Sophia?"

"No, I prefer to learn from Sheffield, if he agrees to my terms."

"Very well, my dear. If at any time you change your mind, do not hesitate to inform me and I will take care of Sheffield. Also, there will be a bell in the room to ring for my assistance."

"Thank you, Belle. I hope you do not think any less of me for agreeing to this preposterous arrangement."

"Nonsense, I am a mistress of the night. It was not so long ago that I was in your position on discovering the hidden emotion of love. If you will follow me, we can progress with the evening."

Sophia followed Belle along the hallway, leading deeper into the privacy of the house. There were no girls hanging in the open doorways. When Belle pushed the door open, it was to find a bedroom as magnificently decorated as the parlor. The walls were painted a dark blue with streaks of white blended in. A makeup stand stood in the corner with bottles of perfume and brushes. Everything a girl would need to prepare for a night of pleasure. Belle walked to a wardrobe that displayed a variety of silken garments. She showed Sophia the bell for assistance. When Belle left, Sophia explored the room. She fell against the mattress and spread out her arms. Her hands stroked back and forth against the softness. Sophia arched her body as she imagined being joined by Sheffield. Was she really going forward on this outrageous agreement? Yes, it would appear she was.

She rose from the bed and discarded her clothing, hiding them in the wardrobe. When Sophia encountered the silky garments, she pulled a few out for inspection. Some were scandalous, bringing a blush to her cheeks. There was no way she could wear these. As her fingers rifled through the sexy lingerie, she found a modest negligee. Sliding the garment over her head, she let the soft blue silk envelope her body. It had slits up both sides of her legs, so when she walked they teased the admirer with her hidden charms. White lace crisscrossed across her breasts with a low vee. Thin straps held the garment on her shoulders. She crossed to the bench and unbound her hair. Brushing it out, she slid some over her left shoulder. When she opened the drawer, she found a selection of masks. She pulled out one with pink silk and pearls decorating the slim apparel. This one didn't tie but clipped to the sides of her hair. Sophia made sure he wouldn't reveal her identity and checked her appearance in the mirror. She stood amazed at the transformation from the prim, proper Sophia to the temptress Violet. Was she one and the same?

She went to the divan near the window and lay down to rest. It surprised her how calm her nerves were. She should be nervous, or at the very least sneaking out to return home. But no, as her eyes drifted shut, she eagerly anticipated his arrival.

Chapter Seven

"You have kept me waiting long enough, Belle. If you did not receive an answer for my request, then you leave me no choice. I will withdraw my membership to your club. Once I leave, others will follow."

Belle smiled as Sheffield continued his rant. She'd decided to make him stew for a while. It served him right, since he'd threatened her. Which only made her delay Sophia's reply longer. Yes, Sophia Turlington had him tied in knots.

"What are you smiling about? Do you not understand that I am threatening your business?"

"Yes, I am quite aware of your empty threats."

"They are not empty."

"We both know they are."

Sheffield sighed as he slumped into her chair, tossing back his drink. The whiskey burned as it slid into his gut. If she didn't have the answer he desired, then there would be more to drink tonight.

"Well?"

"Well what, Your Grace?"

Sheffield scowled. "You damn well know what."

Belle laughed, ready to put him out of his misery. "There are a few conditions you must agree to."

"Anything." He was striding to the door to meet his beauty when the word *conditions* registered. "What? No."

"Yes, or else she will not agree. Then you can continue being your overbearing, demanding self, only to be rejected by a lovely woman. I had the chance to talk with her this afternoon and you are correct. She is divine."

"What do you mean, you talked to her this afternoon? She is one of yours. You've already talked to her."

"No, she isn't one of mine."

"Explain, Belle," he growled.

"Very well. When you brought your request before me, I realized you were not talking about any girl in my employment. You were discussing an innocent lady of the ton. One who called on me to discuss an incident. I'd left her alone to address another problem when *you* seduced her, while under my protection."

"She took part most willing, I assure you."

"Yes, from what I understood from our conversation; she enjoyed your skills in the love-making department."

"Let me get this straight. I have ruined an innocent lady. So, instead of offering a contract for our time together, I should offer for her hand in marriage?"

"Yes, that is what I am suggesting. However, the lady doesn't wish to be wedded to you, only bedded by you. She does not regard you as husband material, but one she could entertain an affair with. And I am apt to agree with her."

"What would be wrong with accepting my hand in marriage? She would be a duchess, one of the highest honors in the realm. She would never want for a thing."

"I do not think she cares two figs for status, only on how her husband would treat her. I think she requires love, something you would lack to give any woman."

"Hah! Love is but a wasted emotion."

"Therefore, she will lie with you, and you need not consider marriage. She realizes she is ruined from your time spent together and wants to enjoy your company again."

"Then why are there stipulations?"

"She wants to keep her identity a secret. She feels if you would discover who she is, you will demand marriage."

"That I will not do. I have already selected the lady I wish to make my bride. Violet won't have to worry that I will force her into a commitment."

"Then you will agree to her terms?"

"If I do, can I visit her this evening?"

"Yes, she is awaiting your answer in one of the private rooms as we speak."

Sheffield came back from the door. "Then yes to all. Now, which room is she in?"

"Do you not want to hear the terms—"

"No, I don't give a damn what they are, as long as I can see her." He turned and opened the door to search the house for Violet.

"Not yet."

Brought up short again he slammed the door and stood angrily against the panel. Would he ever get the chance or was this all a game?

"What are they?"

"First, whenever she changes her mind, you will understand and release her from the agreement." He growled at the first request but agreed, or he would never get to see her. "Second, she will wear a mask at all times.

You will not coax her to remove it, nor will you take it off her face." He nodded. Belle knew the next two requests would make the decision final if he was in agreement.

"Two more, the first is that Violet is a virgin. You have ruined her, and another gentleman has twice." Before Belle could explain the fourth request, Sheffield pounded his fist against the door.

"Who was he?"

"He?"

"Who harmed her? What is the man's name? I will ruin him, and he will wish he never harmed my Violet."

Belle stood in shock at his display of anger. Throughout the entire time she had known Sheffield, he had never portrayed an ounce of anger of any sort. Now here he was threatening to do harm for a lady whose true identity he didn't know. Worse yet, he wanted to harm *himself*. How ironic this farce became. It would also appear Sheffield was even more enamored of Violet than he was prepared to admit. He referred to her as 'mine'. Was he even aware of how he spoke of her?

Belle would have to lie to him.

"I am unaware, Violet did not confide in me the gentleman's name. Only that on two separate occasions he violated her, then spoke to her as if she was nothing."

"No bother, I will speak with Violet about this man."

"Did you hear what I said about her virginity?"

"Yes, and I am honored that she will bestow me with this gift. It clears my mind that no other man has touched her. I will teach her on how I wished to be pleased. The final request?"

"This will only last for one week."

"No."

"Yes, or else you will not spend a minute in her company. Do you agree?"

Sheffield reluctantly accepted again that if he didn't agree, then he would have no stolen moments with her. He would agree for now and try to persuade her later. She would change her mind after they spent time together. He was aware of his charm and his prowess under the bedcovers. He didn't doubt he couldn't talk her into more.

Sheffield bowed before Belle. "Yes. Now, are you going to inform me where I can find her, or do I have to tear your house apart looking for her?"

Belle laughed at his eagerness. Part of her was unsure that she should allow this affair to happen, the other part of her whispered on how it was a match made in heaven. They only needed a gentle nudge to realize they were perfect for each other.

"She is in the midnight room."

"Perfect. Thank you, Belle, for making this possible." Sheffield kissed her on the cheek.

"Do not make me regret this arrangement, Sheffield."

Sheffield nodded as he left. Belle stepped in the hallway and watched as Sheffield hurried to his Violet. She followed at a discreet distance and stared as he stopped in front of the room. He ran his palms along the front of his trousers. Was he nervous? Impossible, the man was too conceited. Belle shook her head as she turned to give the couple the privacy they desired.

Chapter Eight

Sheffield entered the room, expecting … hell, he didn't know what to expect. It wasn't the vision before him though. Violet lay upon the divan on her side, one hand rested underneath her head as she dozed. It was the rest of her that brought him to his knees. The slits in her negligee exposed her legs as it gathered around her thighs. The long length of her legs flashed images of her wrapping them around his hips as he drove into her. He swallowed as his eyes drifted upward to her breasts. They spilled out, the edges of her nipples teasing him. His cock grew into an unbearable hardness. She was exquisite. But it wasn't what he desired to see the most. He needed to see her eyes. He wanted to watch her violet gaze embrace him. To see if her need was as desperate as his.

When he sank to his knees, he wanted to kiss her awake. However, his hands had a mind of their own. They wanted to caress the creamy temptation. His fingers glided over her legs, tracing their softness. When she released a moan, he knew he must touch more of her. He brushed across her nipples. They hardened into tight buds, beckoning his mouth. He lowered his lips, his tongue savoring the sweet nectar. He slid a nipple inside his mouth, softly sucking as his tongue stroked the hard pebble.

His touch slid higher across her soft curls. He teased until her legs spread apart. When he caressed her mound, a soft sound passed her lips. Still, he didn't lift his head but continued to the other nipple. Savoring it between his lips as his fingers sunk into her wetness. He groaned against her and sucked harder as he slipped his finger inside. As he invaded the tight barrier, she caressed his hair. Her touch was light as she coaxed him closer to her chest. With her encouragement he slid another finger inside her tightness, gently stroking in and out. He built a rhythm rapidly out of control, then forced himself to slow down. He remembered Belle's words of her innocence and wanted to make this moment special for her. When he pulled his hand away and lifted his head, he heard her groan in dismay.

Sheffield stared into her dark amethyst depths. Lost in her gaze and the emotions she shared with him, he forgot himself. When her eyes clouded with confusion, he lifted his hands to her cheeks and placed a warm kiss upon her mouth. Gentle, seeking, asking for permission to share his soul. His kisses were light but desperate when their lips pulled away in agony only to seek each other again with every touch.

"Violet," he moaned.

"Yes," she answered in a hesitant whisper.

Sophia awoke to his gentle touch. She had fallen asleep as she waited. When his kisses heated her body, she ached for more. Each stroke held her in a trance, afraid to move in case he would stop. When he put a halt to his caresses, she feared he'd changed his mind. But as soon as he kissed her lips, she understood in her heart he hadn't. His kisses sent her their own message. With each one, she answered his silent questions. He sought permission, and she was more than willing to accept.

"I want to make love to you. You have my promise that I will be gentle with you."

"I trust you will," she spoke in a husky voice she didn't even recognize herself.

"I want it to be special for you, but I don't know if I can. You undo me as no woman ever has."

"You make me feel the same way. Feel my heart beat for you," Sophia told him, guiding his hand over her heart. The steady rhythm beat against their palms.

When he gave her a boyish smile, it was the moment she fell in love with him. She froze, frightened where her thoughts went. Then she settled as she gazed into his eyes. It was there all along, why else would she have agreed to this arrangement? She, Sophia Turlington, was in love with the Duke of Sheffield, Alexander Langley. She wanted to laugh at the ironic situation, but now was not the time to explore her feelings. Now was the time for her to experience the depth of her love for him.

"Sheffield ..."

"Alex, call me Alex."

"Alex."

"What is your true name?"

"Violet," she laughed.

"No, that is my name for you. I want to know who you are."

"No, you promised."

Alex sighed. "Violet it is." For now, he would agree to her secrecy, but he would learn her identity before their time was through.

"You taste like lemons."

"I ate Belle's lemon squares. They're all gone."

"So, you were the culprit."

Sophia blushed. "Oh, were they for you?"

"Yes, my dear. They are my favorite treat. You must pay for depriving me of them."

"How so?" she whispered.

"Mmm, you will have to wait for your punishment," he whispered back as his hands cupped her breasts, his thumbs brushing her nipples as he lowered his head to kiss her neck.

Sophia arched her body into his, aching for more. The whispered words enticing her desire. She no longer cared if this was right or wrong. Or of the consequences, if she were to be caught. To be held in his arms as he stroked her passion was all that rang true through her mind and body.

"You taste like whiskey."

"Do you enjoy the flavor?"

"Mmm, I don't know. I might need to sample more to give a better opinion."

He laughed at her playfulness. His Violet was not only a siren, but a delight to tease. When her laughter joined his, he paused. Her tinkling gaiety soothed him. With everybody else, he had to portray an act of self-righteousness. He had to behave as his title demanded. Even with his closest friend, Wildeburg, he was an ass. However, with her he felt a lightness lift his soul. He sensed his conscience informing him she was the one. The *one*. But his rational side argued, no she wasn't. The circumstances of their union could never come to light. Therefore, this would only be a moment in time to enjoy before it ended. Perhaps the girl was smart for demanding only a week. This way he could get her out of his system. Then move on to finding his duchess.

Sophia's laughter died as she noticed his playful mood turn into reflection. Did she give herself away? She tried to keep her speech husky as Belle had instructed. Did Sheffield recognize her voice? She needed to distract him again. She leaned over to kiss him on the lips, her tongue tracing his. When he opened his mouth, she explored, tasting the whiskey, and savoring the flavor.

"Mmm, yes, most delicious. I could get drunk on your kisses, Alex."

"I am already drunk on you, my sweet Violet."

Alex rose and lifted Violet from the divan to carry her to the bed. The covers were already turned back. With her blonde hair sprawled across the pillows and her eyes filled with desire, he needed to have her now. His eyes traveled the length of her body, taking in her full breasts and long legs. As he continued to stare, he undressed himself. First, he discarded his jacket and vest, letting them fall to the floor. Next went his cravat that he dropped into her hands. She brought the garment to her nose where she breathed in his scent.

His gaze rose to her face, and he watched as she stared at his fingers unbuttoning his shirt. Her eyes grew larger as he took off the garment. When he undid the placket of his trousers, her glance skittered away to the wall. He chuckled at her shyness. When he slid his pants off, her eyes returned. They darkened as he stood before her naked. His cock, hard and aching for her, rose at attention. When her eyes met his, he saw that she held no fear, but a desire as strong as his. With a growl he lowered himself to the bed and stripped the nightgown from her body.

He held her pressed to him. His fingers intertwining in her hair, the only thing in the way was her mask. How easy it would be to slip it from her head, but he wouldn't betray her trust. He didn't want to lose what he only just found. His hands caressed her body as hers did his. Their touches and kisses built their need higher.

Fire consumed Sophia. Every time he uttered the name 'Violet' her senses became enflamed with a need to please him. She was no longer sweet Sophia, but a temptress named Violet. A temptress who wanted to satisfy the hunger of the man who tempted her. Alex. The other half to her soul.

As his kisses consumed her, she slid her hands across his body. She caressed every hardened muscle on his frame. When her hands dipped to his stomach, his body tensed. Then as she brushed across his hardness, he gasped into their kiss. It was then Sophia understood the power she held over him. He was as much enflamed in desire as she was. Her fingers wrapped around his cock, sliding up and down over the smooth velvet skin. His need throbbed at her touch. Her eyes met his again, and she saw his darken with desire. They spoke of his need for her.

Soon, she was underneath him. He gently stroked through her hair. His kiss soft on her lips. A path of fire seared from his hands as he teased her nipples. She moaned and arched her body. He held a hand on her stomach to calm her when she tried to press her hips upwards. Each touch and kiss slowly drew her need to an emotion she didn't know existed. His hands spread her thighs apart and brushed across her wetness, bringing a moan from her lips.

She was ready for him. Her body spoke her need. Every moan and touch from her begged him to take her. However, he wanted to burn each moment into his soul, so that he would never forget their time together. When her leg slid up his body and wrapped around his hip, he was done for. He could wait no longer, he needed to make her his now.

Slowly sliding his cock into her wetness, he paused and looked into her eyes. He expected to see fear, but only saw her desperate need for him. Her gaze was his undoing. He continued inside, pushing past her resistance until he was secure in her soul. Her eyes closed, and he stopped. Afraid that he hurt her. When she opened them again, it was to see her desire turn into a passion unknown to him. He gathered her in his embrace as they made love. Each stroke brought them closer to one another. Her arms wrapped around him holding him close to her heart as her legs tightened, guiding him on. They clung to each other as their bodies burned up their passion for each other.

Sophia was unprepared for the emotions involved in making love. She wanted to cry at the beauty of their souls becoming one. Every time his strokes grew stronger, she cried out for more. She pressed her body into his, driving her hips along with him. She clung to him, weeping his name. He whispered his desires which only enflamed her passion higher.

Alex felt her tighten around his cock and he drove faster. He wanted to send her over the edge with him. When she cried out *Alex*, he only grew harder, needing to brand her with his body. As she clung to him, screaming her pleasure, her wetness coated his cock as he released himself inside her. Her body melted into his and he whispered her name over and over. Violet. Violet. Violet.

Chapter Nine

Sophia rested in a chair near the fire, nursing a cup of tea, as Sidney glared at her from across the room. She'd avoided her friend the last couple of days. Every time Sidney visited her home, Sophia would plead with the servants to lie on her whereabouts. Sophia knew that by not staying at the Hartridge's home she would endure her mother's wrath when her parents returned home. The memories of Sophia's time with Sheffield would help to ease the punishment she would face. Finally, guilt settled in her stomach after she read a note from Sidney. The letter apologized for Sidney's meddling and promised Sophia she only wanted to see her friend that she had missed while away on her honeymoon. So, Sophia visited Sidney during afternoon tea, knowing she would be too busy with visitors as the new Marchioness Wildeburg.

Wilde was explaining, "She only wishes for you to have the same happiness as her."

"Then she needs to stop interfering in my life."

"Those are harsh words. I realize we have not been friends for very long, but your behavior is unlike you."

Sophia rose and wandered to the window away from the other guests. Wildeburg joined her to finish their conversation. She'd thought it would get easier to carry on with her deception, but she found it more difficult to lie to those she loved. Avoiding them in her home was easy, face to face was another story. However, she needed to venture out before suspicion surrounded her. If it wasn't Sidney or Rory calling on her, there was the steady stream of letters requesting her presence at Madame Bellerose. When they first arrived, they were from Belle at the request of Sheffield. Some were private notes from Alex. Each letter more intimate than the one before. They began with concern over her welfare, with the last of them begging for her company. She didn't reply to them, except for the one this morning. Her emotions were too raw to consider meeting him again.

After they made love, he fell asleep with her wrapped in his arms. As she watched him sleep, she saw a vulnerability in him that caused her to fall deeper in love. She slid out of his embrace to dress. Belle assisted with her return home with nobody aware of her absence.

"I apologize, for I am not myself."

"I may not be Sidney, but perhaps I can help you as you helped me."

Sophia's laugh was bitter as she stared out the window. "Nobody can fix the mess I created myself."

He opened the door leading to the terrace and guided Sophia outside away from prying ears. She obviously needed to confide in somebody. When they were out of earshot from his guests, he turned her toward him.

"If the mess you are mentioning is the one concerning Sheffield, then you are not to blame. I will take care of him for you."

Sophia turned toward Wilde, gripping his arm, "No, you shall do nothing of the sort. He has done nothing wrong."

Wilde's eyebrow rose, "Hasn't he?"

"What do you know?"

"Beckwith confided to Sidney and me on how Sheffield accosted you twice. Both of them are seeking vengeance for your virtue."

"Wilde, you must stop them. I do not want a word breathed. There will be a scandal and I won't be forced to wed him. Please, I beg of you."

"Phee, did Sheffield violate you?" Wilde whispered.

"No. No. He ... I cannot explain it to you without you thinking less of me."

"Try."

Sophia raised her head high and closed her eyes, gathering her thoughts before she spoke. She needed to construct her words carefully so that Wilde wouldn't seek Sheffield to harm him.

"Yes, he attempted to kiss me twice. We are both guilty of the kisses spiraling out of control. After he finished kissing me, he spoke a few callous words, and then departed. Nothing more, nothing less."

"Nonetheless, he did not have your permission either time," Wilde growled.

"Well ..."

"Well?"

"Well, not at first, but during maybe." Sophia cringed.

Wilde was furious with Sheffield for taking advantage of Sophia. She was an innocent miss. The next time he encountered Sheffield, he would feel his fury. Better yet, he should take his leave now and approach Sheffield at home. Sophia had become one of his dearest friends, not to mention she was like a sister to his wife. Beckwith had the right idea on destroying the man. As he regarded Sophia, he noticed she wasn't as angry. The entire duration Sheffield courted Sidney, Sophia expressed nothing but distaste for the man. Now she stood before him, begging him to call off Sidney. Wilde grew more confused with the turn of events.

"You care for him."

"Nonsense." Sophia strode ahead, walking down the stairs to the garden.

Wilde followed at a slower pace, allowing her to walk off her frustration. He chuckled to himself at the irony of Sophia Turlington falling for Alexander Langley. They were as different as night and day. Sophia was caring, generous, and always spoke a kind word to everyone. While Sheffield was ... well, Sheffield. An overbearing ass who expected the world to bow down upon his feet. He wanted to guide Sophia away from Sheffield, but it was hopeless judging by her expression. He wondered how Sheffield felt about Sophia.

"Tell me how I can help, Phee."

She turned to stare at him with the saddest eyes. "Can you make him love me?"

"Fallen that hard, have you?" he teased.

"Unfortunately, yes. Pathetic, aren't I?"

"No, my dear, never that."

"I realize this is improper to ask, but can you keep this a secret from Sidney?"

"You know my wife; she will find out, Phee."

"Promise me a few days. Once I sort out my feelings, I will confide in her. Please, until the end of the week."

Wilde nodded his agreement. "I will keep her occupied for a week. Then you are on your own."

"Thank you, Wilde."

"We are friends, Phee, and I still owe you a few."

A voice interrupted them. "This is where they have disappeared to. I was telling Rory how I witnessed my husband abscond with my best friend to the garden and he did not believe me."

"You are correct as always, Lady Wildeburg," Rory laughed.

Sophia turned to her friends with a fake smile plastered on her face. Wilde sent her a wink, promising to keep her secret. However, Sidney noticed the exchange. Nothing ever went by her. Which meant Sidney would question Sophia until she could pacify her with lies.

"If you gentlemen will excuse us, we need some time alone."

Both men bowed to the women and sauntered away. Sophia watched them, aware Sidney would bombard her with questions. She wandered to the bench to sit, knowing it could be a long afternoon. Well, at least with Sidney badgering her, it would keep her thoughts from straying toward Sheffield and the decision she needed to make when she returned home. By now he would have received her message. How he would react, Sophia didn't know.

"I do not know where to begin on offering my apologies for being a miserable friend. But please forgive me. I dislike this distance between us. I miss you," Sidney said.

"You have nothing to beg forgiveness for, Sid. It is I who am a mess. I only ask for your patience while I figure out my thoughts."

"Not for Sheffield?"

"Sid …"

"Anybody but him, Phee."

"Sidney."

"I will stop. Except, from the gossip I hear, he is courting Dallis MacPherson. I don't understand how *you* have fallen for him."

Sophia laughed. "Neither do I, my friend. That is why I plead for your understanding while I decide if Sheffield is the one for me."

"If he is, what then?"

"Then I will expect your help in turn for the guidance I offered to you and Wilde during your so-called courtship."

"When will you make your decision?"

"Give me until Saturday."

"On one condition."

Sophia sighed. She should have known Sidney would not give up so easily. "Only one?"

Sid laughed. "Yes, only one."

"What is your request?"

"You will let me host a dinner party in your honor."

"Is that all?"

"Yes."

"All right, send me an invitation and I shall be here."

"Excellent." Sid hugged Phee.

"I missed you, Phee."

"I missed you too, Sid."

She did too. As an only child, Sophia's mother smothered her with attention. The only peace she had was during her time spent with Sidney. Their mothers were best friends, so her mama always trusted her if she was at the Hartridge's. It would scandalize her mother if she learned her daughter visited a brothel not once, but twice. And on the second visit she gave herself to the Duke of Sheffield. Her mother would chase him to the altar and continue the hunt if she held a clue that her daughter was not only contemplating a third and perhaps a fourth return to Madame Bellerose's establishment. After her talk with Wilde and Sidney, her decision became clear to resume her rendezvous with Alex for the rest of the week. She'd promised him this time together. Also, it would help her to decide if she wanted to share her true affections with him. Was he worth the scandal involved in revealing her identity?

Chapter Ten

Wilde stormed along the hallway leading to Sheffield's study. He shoved the door open, causing it to slam against the wall. The butler, Mason hurried after him, calling for him to stop. When he advanced on Sheffield, Wilde halted when he noticed his friend slouched in his armchair. He held a half-drunken bottle of whiskey to his lips, abusing the fine liquid in a quick swallow. This was a side of Sheffield he had never witnessed, even in their youth when they ran wild. Sheffield always held himself back with an arrogant air from the usual drunken debauchery. Wilde waved Mason away and waited for him to close the door before he approached Sheffield.

While he'd promised Sophia he wouldn't interfere, he owed it to her to defend her honor. She had nobody else. Her parents would demand a marriage contract, and Beckwith couldn't afford to make an enemy out of Sheffield. So, it lay upon him to warn Sheffield away. Marriage to Sheffield would be a miserable affair he wouldn't wish for Sophia to endure.

"What in the hell is wrong with you?"

"Ahh, my good friend Wilde. Back from the honeymoon already?" Sheffield slurred.

"You are drunk."

"Very observant, my good friend. I said that already didn't I? My good friend. Seems like I am repeating myself."

"Because you are, you fool."

"Fool? Am I a fool?"

"Good God, man. What has come over you?"

"Violet."

"Violet?"

"Mmm, yes. She is my temptress, but she hasn't answered my letters the past two days. When she finally did, it was to inform me that she doesn't wish to see me again."

"Who is this Violet?"

Sheffield laughed. "That I do not know. She is a mystery. Can I tell you a secret?"

Wilde sighed. Sheffield was more drunk than he'd first thought. He settled in a chair across from him, grabbing the bottle from Sheffield's grasp. He didn't need to drink any more. Before long he would have to pour coffee down his throat to sober him. The last rumor he heard was that Sheffield courted Lady Dallis MacPherson. Now he was into his cups about a chit named Violet.

"What is your secret?"

"Violet isn't her real name. It is the name I bestowed upon her. She has the most amazing eyes the color of violet that changes shade as her moods alter."

Wilde stilled as Sheffield described his Violet. He knew only one woman who held that eye color. It couldn't be, but Wilde had the weirdest sense it was. Every sign pointed toward the truth of this puzzle. It was an odd shade for an eye color. It would explain Sophia's mixed emotions. But how did Sheffield not realize who his Violet was? Hell, he kissed her twice.

"Where did you meet Violet?"

"Belle's"

"When?"

"The day you had your secret tryst with my intended. While you were bedding Lady Sidney, I became acquainted with this beauty in Belle's parlor."

Now Wilde was more confused than ever—he knew Sophia had waited in the parlor. Why was Sheffield calling her Violet instead of Sophia?

"Her name is Violet?"

"That is what I keep saying, man. Are you not listening?"

"I am only trying to understand your story. Please carry on."

"She is a beauty like no other."

"Is she a new girl of Belle's?"

"No, no, no. You married my fiancé, Violet is mine. Nobody will taste her treasures, but I."

"If she is Belle's, then many will sample her treasures."

"No," Sheffield roared as he tried to rise, but his unsteadiness caused him to fall back in a slump against the chair cushions.

"Explain who Violet is. I am confused."

"You will not request her from Belle's?"

"Sheffield, I am a married man and no other woman will ever hold my interest except for Sidney. Your Violet is safe from me."

"Nobody else will touch her. She is mine and as soon as I can convince her, she will be forever."

"You intend to make her your duchess?"

"No. Violet could never be my duchess with the scandal surrounding our relationship. No, I will keep her as my mistress. I plan to make Lady Dallis MacPherson my intended."

If he was correct on the identity of the elusive Violet, then Sheffield would soon be disappointed.

"Will she agree?"

"With the right persuasion I am certain she will."

Wilde took a drink from the bottle. He wanted more, but needed his senses about him to tackle this new dilemma. He was positive Sophia was Violet. After he left, he would make a stop at Belle's for the full story. Then he would have to explain this mess to his wife without her inserting her way into the drama. He rose and went to the door, calling for the butler and ordering coffee for Sheffield. Returning to the chair he watched Sheffield, who had his eyes closed, muttering to himself.

When Mason delivered the coffee, he held a missive toward Sheffield. The letter was enclosed in a decorative envelope with purple flowers and a feminine script. He recognized the stationary, for Sidney had received many with the same design in the last week. Sophia had avoided Sidney since they met in the park, but written often. His suspicions were now confirmed.

Sheffield grabbed the letter and sat straighter in the chair. As his eyes devoured the words, he instantly sobered. She wanted to meet him this afternoon. Now, in fact. He needed to make himself presentable before he saw her again. The aroma of coffee drifted toward him. He should drink a few cups, but decided not to. Violet loved the flavor of whiskey when she kissed him.

"I must leave. You will see yourself out, won't you?"

"Violet?"

"Yes, she requests my company."

"Should you not drink your coffee before you meet her?"

Sheffield laughed. "No."

"Well, then. I bid you goodbye and wish you the best of luck with your Violet."

Already entranced with reading the letter again, Sheffield was unaware that Wilde left. He thought he'd lost her after their night together.

When he awoke at Belle's and she'd disappeared, he felt a sense of loss deep in his soul. Then, as she refused to meet him, he became desperate. His need for her consumed his life. Her missive this morning conveyed her regrets that she needed to break their arrangement. They would only have the one evening spent in each other's arms. But as he read this letter, she expressed her fears to him and wanted to share what precious time they had remaining for the week.

Only it would be longer than that. He would not scare her away with his requests today. But by the end of their affair, she would be his for eternity. There would be no way she would refuse him.

~~~~~~

Belle greeted him, "Wilde, my darling. You are a sight for sore eyes. How are you enjoying married life to the enchanting Sidney?"

"It is beyond my wildest dreams."

"What do I owe this lovely visit to? I cannot imagine it is for the services of my girls."

Wilde laughed. "No, you will send them my regrets. I believe you know why I am here. Did you not think I wouldn't learn about the latest development brewing in your home?"

"You know?"

"Bits and pieces. I hoped you could fill in the rest. I need to hear the complete story before my wife gets wind of this mess."

"Have a seat, Wilde, and let me pour you a drink. This may take a while."

"My first question is, why, Belle?"

"She is the one for him, Wilde. They are soul mates and need a small push toward one another."

"You are aware that if this scandal comes to light, your establishment will have to close."

"If he finds happiness, it will be worth it."

"He plans to ask her to be his mistress for life."

"There is no way she can."

"I realize that and so do you, but he is under the assumption he can change her mind."

"She will never agree; the arrangement is only for this week."

"Please start from the beginning."

Belle explained to Wilde how Sophia became unattended on the day he spent with Sidney. During that time, Sheffield became enamored of Sophia and requested time spent alone with her. Belle told Wilde how she'd debated if the two should meet. But after a long talk with Sophia she decided they needed to explore the feelings they shared. She developed an arrangement that Sophia and Sheffield agreed upon. One stipulation was that Sophia would wear a mask to hide her identity. Sheffield agreed, and the rest was history.

"Sophia will get hurt."

"I fear they both will. You should see him, Wilde, he is in love with her."

"I just came from his house, Belle. Sheffield is obsessed with her. I doubt those emotions are the same as love."

"Trust me, they are."

"I hope for everyone's sake, you are correct."

Belle reflected on Wilde's thoughts. She knew in her heart she was correct. But they needed to be honest with one another. Sheffield must see Sophia as his duchess. Maybe if they spent time as Sheffield and Sophia, they could discover the same magic.

"Perhaps, your wife could draw them together in a setting for Sheffield to experience Sophia's charm."

Wilde shook his head. There was no way Sidney would understand this. Her protective instincts would come alive and Sheffield would never be safe to set foot in London, let alone England, after Sidney was through with him.

Belle watched the doubt cross his face and dropped the subject. This *would* require the devious mind of Sidney Hartridge. No, Sidney Wildeburg to accomplish the result of happily ever after for Sheffield and Sophia. Belle would send an invitation for Sidney to join her for tea tomorrow. Then they could devise a plan for the couple to be together forever.

However, she said, "Yes, it would be best not to involve your lady. Give me time to think of a way to end their arrangement."

"You have one week before I end this farce on my own terms. Her parents are out of town at their estate. Once they return, if this hasn't finished on its own accord, then by the hand of her father—or should I say her mother—it will."

"You have my promise."

Wilde rose and brushed a kiss across Belle's cheek. "I am going home to my bride."

"Give Sidney my love."

Belle watched as Wilde left before she called for Ned. Upon her instructions, he left to do her bidding. Belle knew the drama would soon unfold in her home and among the ton, but it couldn't make her any happier. Before long she would have a cohort to help her guide two lost souls to happiness.

Chapter Eleven

Sheffield waited impatiently in their room for her arrival. She was late. Did she change her mind? He paced back and forth in front of the windows. Every time he heard the clomps of horses' hooves he looked out, hoping to catch a glimpse of his beauty. Only to be disappointed time and time again. He stared as another carriage conveyed along the street. He leaned his head against the glass and closed his eyes. When the click of the doorknob turned, he glanced over his shoulder to see her standing in the doorway. Her fingers twisting in front of her nervously. She came. He swung around and their gazes locked. She appeared hesitant as if she would change her mind at any moment.

Before she had a chance to leave, he rushed toward her. Sheffield swung her into his arms and shut the door behind them as his lips met hers. All hesitation disappeared when their lips connected. As he carried her to the bed, she wrapped her hands around his neck drawing his head closer. Her shy kisses spoke of her desire for him. He felt a punch in his gut at the need he held for her. He let her control their passion. They were soft and slow. Each kiss drawn out into a powerful tide. The innocent touch of her tongue as she guided his lips apart undid him. She stroked inside his mouth, tasting him. Soon her tongue clashed with his, and the kiss took a turn. From innocent exploration to a desire so strong they clung to one another.

"You taste like whiskey again. Do you drink a lot, Sheffield?"

"Only when I am desperate for the flavor of you."

"Oh." Sophia didn't know how to respond to such a bold statement.

"Now I can get drunk on you."

Sophia blushed at his boldness. Soon, her blushes disappeared as she became consumed by his kisses and the strokes of his hands as he caressed her. He slowly stripped her dress off, kissing her exposed skin as he went. There was not a spot on her body that he didn't devour. When he discarded her clothing, she lay underneath him naked to his gaze. When she saw the desire darken his eyes, she imagined herself as a goddess. She stretched her arms above her head and noticed his eyes lingered on her breasts as they lifted higher. When her eyes raked his body, she saw his cock straining against his trousers and knew that he wanted her too.

She rose to her knees and crawled to the edge of the bed, "You are overdressed, Your Grace."

"Alex," he growled.

Sophia started to undress him. Her lips leaving the same trail as his. Every piece of garment she removed, her lips branded his soul. She was a minx. Her fingers teased as they stroked across his chest. When her kisses followed the path, he knew he wouldn't last long. As she undid his trousers and slid them down over his buttocks, her small hands wrapped around his cock. When she lowered her body and slid her tongue across the tip, his knees buckled. The touch of her lips on him was heaven. No, he would not last if she continued this torture. However, he did. Her tongue stroked along the length, tasting him. When her mouth enclosed and slid him inside her mouth, he grasped her head and held her to him as she softly sucked. He became harder with each kiss, suck, and lick inside her mouth.

He pulled her away. "You must stop, my dear."

"Why?" she inquired with a look filled with innocence.

"Because …" he couldn't continue since she ignored his plea.

Sophia was aware of why she should stop, but she didn't want to. She wanted to savor the very essence of Alex. When she'd opened the door and saw his desperate look as he gazed out the window, her heart soared. No words she read ever described the feelings she experienced now. The powerful emotions coursing through her body as she pleased him urged her to finish loving him. To offer him the pleasure, as he did to her, enhanced her love for him.

Her tongue stroked his cock as she slid him in and out of her mouth. When he throbbed and hardened, she knew he was close to exploding. She wanted to give him this ultimate gift before she ended their time together. When he slid his hands through her hair and moaned the name of his desire, 'Violet', part of her was saddened to not hear Sophia. But another part encouraged the temptress in her to be the woman she desired to be. Open to love. As her tongue circled the tip of his cock, licking off his wetness, she slowly slid her mouth down the length of him and sucked until he exploded, screaming her name.

Alex gathered Violet in his arms and held her, whispering her name as his body calmed from the aftershocks. However, his Violet was feisty. Her torture never ended. She placed soft kisses all over his body, soothing him. When her lips hovered over his, their eyes met. Connecting.

"Kiss me."

At first Sophia thought it was an order. As their gazes never broke, she began to understand it was not a command, but a desperate declaration. His eyes begged for her to kiss him. Sophia wrapped her palms around his cheeks. Lowering her head, she placed a gentle kiss on his lips. Sweet kisses filled with passion.

Her kisses invaded his soul, slow and gentle, as her lips teased him. He opened his mouth under hers, letting her guide the passion. Each kiss slower than the one before, drawing out their desires. He became lost in her gaze. He rolled her over, nestling her body underneath his. Their legs entangled as he brought her closer against him. Her softness melting into his rough exterior. His lips left hers to wander down her neck, moving lower to her breasts. His hands molded her creamy globes in his grip. When his tongue licked across her nipples, she arched her body into his. As he drew her nipple between his lips, he softly sucked it into a hard pebble. He teased the bud with his tongue as his hand lowered between her legs. She opened them wide for him. As his finger slid into her wetness, she arched her hips wanting more. His head lowered kissing across her stomach as his fingers moved, drawing her passion tight. His head rose to meet her eyes behind the mask, to watch them darken into his favorite shade.

Sophia waited in anticipation for his next move. She knew what he was about to do and trembled for his kiss. Her eyes met his, and she saw his intent and desire. She lifted her hands to slide through his thick black hair for encouragement. With a growl, his lips descended to her core where he assaulted her senses with his passion. She moaned in delight as the sensations took over her body. His mouth made love to her, each kiss and stroke of his tongue sending her to a higher level.

Oh, his Violet tasted better than he could ever have imagined. Sweet, exotic wetness glided over his tongue sliding inside her, stroking her passion higher. Her body shook beneath his hands. As his mouth loved her, he brushed his thumb across her clit, stroking. She lifted her hips higher as he drove her over the brink. Each kiss became stronger as his fingers worked their magic. When her hands gripped his head as she screamed his name, his mouth claimed her wetness as his. The shudders that had racked her body calmed as he held her in his arms.

Alex gently kissed her lips. When the storm calmed in her eyes, he declared, "You are mine and I will allow no other to have you."

"Shh," she whispered as she pressed a finger to his lips. "Love me, Alex."

Alex rose above her as he slid inside her. Slow. So that she could feel every inch of him as he entered her. She responded by wrapping her legs around his hips as she matched his rhythm. Slow. Each stroke drawing out their need for each other. Slow. Each touch and kiss precious for fear of breaking the other. Slow.

When she tightened around his cock and exploded, he fell with her. Deep into the passion only they shared. With his arms wrapped embracing her, he settled her head onto his chest as his fingers threaded through her hair. Her ribbon caught his ring and urged him to pull it loose. Only he didn't. He didn't want this fantasy to end. He only wanted her love, not her anger. However tempting it might be.

He felt her body relax against him in sleep. This time he wouldn't rest, for he wanted to speak with her instead of having her escape on him. When he slid her over, she fell back into the pillow. Not once did he take his gaze off her as she slept. Once again, as his eyes devoured her innocence, calm entered his soul.

~~~~~~

Sophia awoke to a pair of eyes staring at her. The grin on his face, as she awakened, she would cherish in her heart forever.

"You look younger when you smile. Why don't you smile more often?"

"Nothing else brings me joy in life."

"You were recently engaged. Did that not make you happy?"

"You know of my engagement?"

Sophia nodded, not wanting to divulge any more information for fear of giving herself away.

"Then you know why I am no longer engaged."

"Yes. I have also heard about your quest to find a new duchess. Have you narrowed your choices?"

"I have." This conversation made him feel uneasy. He listened to the sorrow in her voice. He needed to change the topic before he blurted out his intentions for her.

"Is it to be Lady Dallis MacPherson?"

"Yes."

"Oh." A sadness overcame her eyes as she averted them from his gaze.

Damn. Why couldn't he have met her under different circumstances? Obviously, she was a member of the ton who knew of his standing. Perhaps someone in his close circle. Now, after their time spent together, they could never be. Scandal surrounded their involvement. He watched as a tear leaked down her cheek from behind the mask.

"Don't," he moaned as he rested his forehead against hers, staring into her eyes. "Please don't."

"Don't what?"

"Cry."

Which only made her cry more. It was all so unfair. It didn't make sense how they shared an intimacy as Alex and Violet, yet when they met outside as Lady Sophia and the Duke of Sheffield, they never spoke one kind word to each other. How could he hold her as a precious gift one moment, then the next time they meet, make snide remarks toward her?

Alex gathered Violet in his embrace and held her as she cried her sorrows at their predicament. After her tears dried, he started talking to her. He asked what her favorite things were; flowers, books, and treats. Anything to distract Violet from the sorry state of their affair. They discussed the similarities between them as single children. He explained the high expectations that were demanded because of his title. He revealed his true passions, a part of him Sophia held not a clue about.

She spoke of her love of reading romance novels. He asked if that was how she learned her expertise on pleasing him. With a blush spreading over her body, she admitted to the erotic novels she found at a certain bookstore. Alex whispered what he could teach her, and that she didn't need to read about them. Then he proceeded to show her during the rest of the evening and into the next morning his knowledge on making love.

~~~~~~

"Love, do you need to return home to your parents?" He kissed her shoulder as he leaned over her.

"Mmm," Sophia moaned into the pillow.

"Violet?"

Sophia rolled over to regard Alex through her drowsy eyes. Disappointment flooded her when she saw him next to the bed, already dressed and ready to leave for the day.

"I must be off. I will have Belle arrange a carriage for your return home."

"No bother, I shall reside here this week."

"How will you explain this arrangement to your family? I do not wish for a scandal, my dear. While I love bedding you, I will not wed you. Do not think to trap me."

And once again he was the arrogant duke she despised. He only considered himself and not others. Why Sophia loved him was beyond her. Her anger got the best of her as she unleashed her fury at his conceited ego. She pushed him away as she rose from the bed with the sheet wrapped around her body. She spilled her thoughts out loud, ticking them off on her fingers as her voice grew louder.

"First, I will not have to explain this arrangement to my family, because an emergency at the family estate called for my parent's attention. Second, there will be no scandal involving you or our time together. Third, while I love bedding you also, I do not believe I have even hinted at wanting to be married to an overbearing, egotistical ass such as yourself. Fourth, I have no intention of trapping you into anything but the use of your body for the remainder of the week. Furthermore, let me make myself clear, I am too good for the likes of you. One day a ring shall be placed upon my finger, but only by a man who deserves me, and that man is not you. Now, if you will be so kind, please leave my bedroom now."

Sophia finished her tirade standing at the door, pulling it open for him to leave. She watched as he stood across the room, glaring at her. Her foot tapped in annoyance the longer he stood there. If he didn't leave soon, she would rip off her mask to reveal her identity. Then he could deal with who she was and how, if she wanted to trap him, she could. Her father was a powerful man in the ton. If she cried injustice at the hands of the Duke of Sheffield, he would make the duke beg for her hand in marriage.

Sheffield walked over to stand before her, staring at his wild temptress in her fit of anger. He didn't know whether to be furious with her for addressing him in that tone, or to carry her to the bed and make love to her all day. She riled his emotions on another level. As she stood before him, the sheet slipped from her grasp as she pointed at the door for him to leave. Her tangled hair fell over her shoulders hiding her breasts from his gaze. Her body shook in anger as she continued to glare at him with those dark violet eyes that shot sparks of silver at him. While he would love to stay and turn them into passion, he was already late for an appointment. But he had time to kiss her and show her just how arrogant he was.

He pulled her into his arms and her glare intensified as she dared him to kiss her. He wore the smirk of a man who takes a dare and declares himself the winner.

Sophia knew from his stare that he wanted to ravish her lips and she would be powerless to stop him. Because angry as she was, she still desired him. Sophia wanted him to kiss her, then it would mean he desired her too. However, when his lips lowered to hers, it was the kiss of an apology. Soft. Slow. Gentle. Each brush of his lips against hers asked for forgiveness.

He meant to ravish her and stake his dominance, however when his lips met hers, it was to ask for forgiveness. So, he kissed his apology upon her lips. With each stroke of his tongue he begged for her forgiveness. When she responded with her own gentle strokes, he felt in his heart she had forgiven him. With one final touch of his lips on hers he pulled away and stepped back. He bowed as if she was a queen, then walked out of the room and along the hallway. When he rounded the corner, he stopped. He stood there with his breath held until the door clicked shut. Alex leaned his head against the wall and closed his eyes as he brought himself under control. Walking away from her was the hardest thing he ever did. However, it was for the best.

They were two individuals whose tempers flared in a moment of passion. He didn't want to ruin what time he had remaining by fighting. Already he'd soured it with his outburst on trapping him into a marriage. He would have to confess his problem and make her understand why he needed to marry Lady Dallis MacPherson. Then he would persuade Violet to be his mistress. It was his only chance not to lose her. Also, she'd betrayed some information to her identity in her fury. He must keep his ears open at society functions on which peer was called away from town to their estate. Perhaps he would follow her and learn just who was his mysterious Violet? Then she wouldn't need to wear a mask and they could be free in their relationship.

Maybe he could even find another respectable gentleman to marry her, one who lived close to his own estate.

Once he settled his thoughts, Sheffield left Belle's and returned home.

~~~~~~

Belle listened to the raised voices coming from Sophia's room. She hesitated in the hallway, wondering if she should interrupt. When they quieted, and she heard footsteps walking along the hallway, she ducked into a room. She watched as Sheffield halted when he stepped around the corner. He appeared unsure of himself; Belle noticed how he tried to calm his emotions. The door to Sophia's room closed. The pair appeared to have had a disagreement of sorts. Sheffield opened his eyes and continued away. A smile graced Belle's face seeing that Sophia had wedged herself deeper into his heart.

Belle slipped from her hiding place and walked to the front parlor where an important guest was waiting. When she entered, it was to find the marchioness seated and pouring tea. Lady Sidney wore a cunning smile at Belle's entrance. Belle returned her smile as she sat across from her.

Sidney said, "I am assuming from your letter and my husband's confession; my friend resides in your home this week."

"He confessed already? He said he would give it the week it required."

"Yes, well I can be very persuasive."

"I'm sure you can."

"Were the raised voices I overheard them?"

"Yes, they were."

"And my friend is well?"

"Yes, I believe so. I think *my* friend stirred your friend's temper into a snit."

"He has the tendency to draw out her frustrations. Do you think we can coax them into a more amicable relationship?"

"Do we need to? I think it gives the right spark to their explosion."

"I believe you are correct. Since you are aiding them with the scandal to bring them together, how may I be of assistance?"

"Would you be able to draw them together in more innocent meetings? Perhaps a dinner party, or you can persuade him to dance with her at a ball. Small interactions to draw his attentions to her charms outside of the bedroom."

"It will be difficult." Sidney thought for a while. "I think I shall attempt an experiment of sorts."

"Do you have a plan?"

"An idea comes to mind. I shall use a technique that I used on my research which landed me Wilde."

"And that is?"

"Why, good old-fashioned jealousy," Sidney laughed.

Chapter Twelve

Over the next couple of days they settled into a strange courtship. Alex would send Sophia gifts, small trinkets at first. A box of candy, a bottle of perfume, then he started sending her books. First a simple gothic romance, then a few books from his personal library. More of the erotic kind, and he would place bookmarks in the novels sharing his favorite passages. When she read them, she blushed. When he acted out the scenes, she moaned in pleasure begging to learn more.

There was no more talk about his quest to find a bride, or her anger toward him. They avoided the sensitive subjects for more intimate acts. Their time was limited, and they explored their relationship with a desperate need. They feared the week coming to an end. Between their love-making they discussed their passions and dreams. Each of them discovered a layer of personality they would never have expected from the other. Sophia discussed her passion for the unfortunate and the need to help educate them. Alex shared his secret charity of helping orphans. When he explained how he supported two orphanages in the east end of London near the docks, her heart opened wider for him. He told her how he hired tutors to teach the children and supplied them with apprenticeship opportunities for their future. If any child was caught pick-pocketing or exploiting themselves, he would send them on their way. Their interests were so similar it was uncanny. How their activities never crossed as members of the ton astonished her. She'd never heard whispers of his unselfish efforts.

Every night he arrived to share a small meal with her. Not only at nights, but during the day he would surprise her with his company for lunch. The majority of the time they spent resting on the divan while he held her in his embrace, sharing secrets. However, this evening would be different. She noticed the difference in him after he entered. His eyes were alight with a need the moment he walked into the bedroom. He prowled through the door, determined for an evening of passion. One Sophia anticipated with her own desire.

He wanted her with a passion stronger than he could contain. Their time together this week only strengthened their bond of intimacy. While he enjoyed their long conversations, and her excitement when he brought her gifts, it didn't compare to when he held her in his arms and made love to her. His surprises for her tonight would only enhance the memories they would share in the future. When he entered the room, he found Violet standing at the window.

The other times he visited her a simple day-dress graced her form. However, this evening a nightgown of violet adorned her body. The dark silk emphasized the color of her eyes. The soft material draped her body, a long slit up one side of her leg, and her breasts spilled from the deep vee of her gown. Her long blonde hair hung along her back with a few curls dangling near her breasts, teasing him to wrap around his finger. She stood waiting for his reaction. The only thing running through his brain was to slide the silk up her legs and take her against the window now. His need for her controlled all his thoughts and emotions. But his desire to please her with more gifts overruled his need to claim her. He wanted to present her tonight with his plans for their future. He must remain calm and in control, for he knew she would put up resistance to his ideas. Tonight was otherwise their last moment together. It had been a week.

Sophia watched as he hurried over and halted near the bed, his hand holding the bedpost in a death grip. She continued to stare as he tried to rein in his passion. Confused, she took a step toward him. His grasp tightened, turning his fingers red. She was eager for his touch and needed him now. Tonight would be their last evening together and she didn't want to waste a moment not being held in his arms. She wanted him to make love to her throughout the night. Belle had helped to choose a new negligee to match her eyes. Sheffield must never forget Violet. Her footsteps advanced again. A light growl hummed between his lips and his hand turned white against the strain of his grasp. Sophia smiled at him knowingly.

Alex stared as her confusion transformed into the smile of a siren. She finally understood the power she wielded. If she touched him, all his plans for the evening would fly out the window. He was powerless to her charm.

"Alex," she purred.

Her husky voice whispering his name slipped his control lower. He gulped as her hand reached out to run across his chest, rubbing in small circles. As she came closer, he inhaled the fragrance he gifted her yesterday. The exotic scent stamped a memory into his soul. Whenever he breathed it again, he would remember her. As his eyes drifted lower, he gulped again as her breasts spilled from her gown, her nipples teasing his vision and begging for him to kiss them. He took a step backward.

"Alex," she purred again, and this time her hand traveled to the placket of his trousers.

He grabbed her hand, enclosing her fingers and brought them to his mouth. He placed a kiss on them, shaking his head in denial. Her lips pouted her disappointment, his innocent temptress now a devilish siren meant to lead him down a path of sensual pleasure. He almost blurted out a marriage proposal in that instant. To hell with the scandal, or if she was even duchess material. It no longer mattered. When she stood on her toes and pressed her lips to his and pulled away to rest on the divan, it was clear what a mistake that would have been. His life outside of this house lay in shambles and he couldn't afford any mistakes. This week was a whim he would never regret, but he must make other arrangements to avoid a scandal.

Sophia by now understood Sheffield. She could tell how he held on to his passions with a tight restraint and almost fell into her arms, but hesitated for a reason. He was a practical man who always had a plan. He would not give into the temptation until he was ready. She was tempted to entice him to loosen his stiff exterior. However, she also wanted to learn the purpose of his seriousness.

So, she rested on the divan, laying out in a tempting pose. She watched as emotions flittered across his face as she waited for his reaction. She shifted her legs, causing the slit in her nightgown to open wider, displaying the full length of her bare leg. He moved one step toward her. She ran her fingers across her chest, sliding her hair off to the side. Two steps closer. Her tongue slid out to trace her lips, biting her lower lip as she waited. Soon he stood above her. When she tilted her head against the pillow, his eyes darkened to the deepest shade of blue she had ever seen. She gulped at the power of emotions spilling forth from the depth of his gaze. It was then Sophia realized she was playing with fire, a fire that would only consume her. Up to now he had only singed her; tonight would be a burn from which she would never recover.

He trapped her with his stare, declaring his full desires. She had nowhere to retreat. She'd teased him to this point. Now all he could do was give in to her. Be damned with his plans for this evening. No part of their relationship was the standard courtship. It had been explosive from the start.

He didn't need to be the Duke of Sheffield. He only needed to be Alex. So, Alex she would have. His plans for them would come later when they burned the fire that heated the room, consuming them at this moment.

He dropped to his knees. "Violet," he moaned as he took her lips in a kiss full of the passion simmering between them.

She responded by wrapping her arms around him and welcoming him into her hold. Finally, her wish would be granted. She had wondered if she held this power over him and felt relieved that she did. She didn't want to use it, but only wished to know if she held any.

Their lips met in a fiery explosion from their bent-up passion. Each kiss overwhelming their need for more. He tasted of whiskey and soon she would taste of lemon after his surprise. For now, the flavor of Violet was enough for him. She would always be enough for him. Their hands removed their clothing. Each touch urgent and full of need. He pulled her off the couch and seated himself against the cushion, drawing her on top of him. He guided her hips as he slid his cock inside her wetness. Her body already throbbed with her desire. He watched the purple depths darken as she enjoyed their new position. Each moment he taught her something new, she responded as no woman he had ever known.

Their new position shocked Sophia, but the enjoyment she felt turned her astonishment to exploration. She rose as she felt his cock sliding out of her, then swiftly lowered. Hearing his groan of pleasure, she repeated her actions and the next time she rotated her core against his cock. He gripped her hips as his fingers stroked their pleasure at her movements.

She was heaven and hell in his arms at this moment. Her curiosity always enflamed his desire, but this was on a whole new level. Every time she rose and fell, his cock throbbed inside her tightened core. Her wetness slid between their bodies with every stroke. He knew she was ready; she held on for him. When she lowered her mouth to kiss him, long and slow, he gripped her hips tighter and rose into her. Matching her rhythm, he sent them into the burning fire together. He brought her back against the cushions with him, wrapping her in his embrace. As her body quieted in his arms, he stroked her hair and whispered words of endearments. After their trembles ceased, he kissed the top of her head.

"You ruined my plans for the evening, my dear."

She chuckled. "I was trying to. You were much too serious for my mood, Your Grace."

"Alex," he growled.

"Alex," she sighed, pulling back and propping her hands on his chest, resting her chin atop them.

He regarded the amusement in her eyes. His hands hovered over her hair, debating to untie those knots again. When her gaiety turned into panic at his intentions, he lowered his hands to run along her cheeks. Her violet eyes changed to hesitation. She feared him knowing who she was. It was then he knew his plans for their future would never be. Her identity would remain a mystery. The only way for him to discover who she was would be to follow her when she left Belle's for the final time. To do that would betray all the trust she gifted him with this past week. Would abusing her trust to live a life of scandal be worth it? All he knew was that he could never hurt her. If he followed her, that would upset her. He decided to sacrifice his desires for her happiness. As much as it tore at his heart, he finally understood that when he left this room, their time must end.

Their awkward moment was interrupted by a knock on the door. A relief, for he could continue to spoil her with his surprises. After they parted ways, he could reflect on the treasures she gifted him with. He rolled off the divan, laying a cover over her naked form. Before he opened the door, he slid on a robe and guided servants into the bedroom. Candlelight flickered across the room and on the table with covered dishes. When the last of the servants departed, Alex locked the door and continued to her side with her new violet wrapper in his hands. He guided her into the garment and held her in his embrace. After he seated her at the table, he handed her a single white rose. She lifted the flower to her nose and smiled at his simple gesture.

"Now, my dear, I have had Belle's chef prepare a dinner with all your favorites."

Sophia giggled at his explanation and then laughed even harder as he lifted the lids to the platters. All her favorite desserts. Every pie she loved, different flavors of cake, biscuits, and a wide variety of pastries. One dish stayed covered. Her curiosity prompted her to lift the lid. However, his hand stopped her. He shook his head with a smile.

"That is the dessert of all desserts. First you must eat your dinner, then you can have a bite."

"You are being unfair, please give me a hint."

"Mmm, lemon. That is all I will reveal."

"Mmm, I love lemon."

"I know, my love."

The endearment hung in the air between them. Neither one of them questioned why he spoke the intimate words. Sophia wished them to be true. Alex had expressed them out of necessity. He wanted her to know how she'd touched his heart during their arrangement.

Sophia ate, not wanting those sentiments to sink too deeply. She knew he spoke them out of context, yet it still hurt. Was there any truth to them? Instead of asking, she filled a plate with the delicious morsels.

Alex saw the doubt in her eyes. He wanted to shout out his love, but held the emotion deep inside his heart. She moaned over the delight of his treats. He teased her, and they settled into an easy banter over their enjoyment of dinner. Each regaling the other with moments in their childhood. He learned of her friend that she valued as a sister. He envied her friend, wishing it to be him. However, it gave him comfort that she had someone to confide in who wouldn't shun her. Sheffield had blundered his friendship with Wilde, and after his time with Violet he understood his friend's quest for Sidney. Wilde must have been as enamored with Sidney as Sheffield was of Violet. Perhaps Wilde could help him deal with his latest predicament. He meant to share his troubles with Violet, but now realized they could never be.

After Sophia sampled every delicious treat, she reached for the last tray. She glanced at Alex, whose smile spread wide as he waited for her reaction. She lifted the lid and her mouth watered at the scrumptious treat. It was a lemon concoction in between butter biscuits. Scoops of whipped cream lay in layers of lemon pudding. She squealed in delight as she lifted her spoon to slide into the dessert. She brought the spoon to her lips. When she closed her eyes, the tart lemon flavor exploded her senses, with the whipped cream soothing the sour within her mouth. Her moans drew chuckles from Alex. It was divine. No dessert had ever tasted so sweet.

"You spoil me, Alex."

"You are meant to be spoiled, my sweet Violet."

"Mmm," she moaned between bites. She took a biscuit and dipped it into the lemon. More moans escaped as she had a taste.

Alex watched her enjoyment. He groaned as her tongue licked the sweet lemon pudding off the biscuit. His need for her had never diminished, and it only grew stronger as she sucked each finger. She settled herself on his lap and gave him lemon-flavored kisses. Each kiss was as tart as the one before.

"You taste like lemon."

"A flavor to imprint on your mind to always remember me by."

"You will be impossible to forget, regardless of lemons."

She lifted the spoon to his mouth to sample the treat. While she loved hearing his thoughts on never forgetting her, they were too much to bear. She wanted to keep their evening lighthearted and full of passion. He took the bite and closed his eyes as he enjoyed the dessert. A love of lemon treats was another thing they shared in common. When he opened his eyes, they were filled with his need for her again. He untied her robe and slipped the gown over her shoulders, her breasts displayed for his pleasure. When he dipped his fingers into the lemon and smoothed the creamy dessert across her nipples, she realized his full intention for the treat.

Alex's lips slid down to lick the pudding off, each stroke of his touch savoring her tartness. As he sucked the lemon sweetness between his lips her buds tightened in his mouth. She moaned her delight at his attention, and he wanted to try more.

By now, nothing should shock her about Alex's passion. However, he kept her surprised with new ways to love her. Even the books he supplied for her curiosity never did justice to his ideas. He lowered her to the bed and showed why he'd ordered the special dessert. He licked the lemon pudding off every inch of her body and in return she bestowed the same favor upon him. This time laughter filled their love-making. Every stroke of the tongue or smearing of lemon teased and tickled, enhancing their passion. As they lay in each other's arms, they expressed their humor with more laughter at the stickiness of their bodies.

Alex rose and called the servants, ordering a bath and a change of the bed sheets. Sophia moved into the changing room, embarrassed at the mess they created. He chuckled and teased her until her body glowed red. Which only brought forth more laughter from him. When the servants left, he coaxed her to join him in the tub. As she pressed her back against him, he soaked her body. His touch gentle as he wiped the lemon concoction away. Her hair lay in rivulets against his chest. He lifted it from her nape to wash away more of the dessert. There he discovered a small mole underneath her hairline and placed his lips upon her imperfection. Another treasure to mark the beauty of his Violet. Her body relaxed against his as she dozed in the warm water. Not wanting to disturb her sleep he continued to wash them of their stickiness. When he finished, he carefully held her. The simplicity of the moment soothed him, although their time was ending. As the water chilled, he rose with her in his arms and settled them between the clean sheets. The whole time his Violet never stirred. He wished to wake her and make love to her before he left, but he didn't want to disturb her slumber. There would be time in the morning for him to love her goodbye. Before he drifted off to sleep, he took a gift from his jacket pocket. It was supposed to persuade Violet to continue their union—his plans now scratched since she would never agree. He lifted the locket over her neck. As it nestled between her breasts, he placed a soft kiss across her lips and whispered words of love into the darkness.

~~~~~~

Sophia awoke as the sun began to rise, her body wrapped tightly in Alex's arms. His grip even in sleep wouldn't relinquish her. She'd been aware of his intentions when he entered the room the evening before. He meant to ask her to continue their arrangement, with a house in the country. Belle had informed Sophia of Sheffield's plans while she'd helped with the new nightgown. Sophia could never agree to such an outlandish request. The scandal alone would embarrass Sheffield. She couldn't hurt him with her true identity. No, it was best they part ways.

The hardest thing she did was to untangle herself from his arms. As she dressed to depart, she watched him. He mumbled her name as he reached for her. With a hushed whisper to soothe him, he settled back to sleep. Tears slid from her eyes as she stood watching him rest. Her bags were already waiting for her below. Belle would have Ned escort her home as discreetly as possible. Her time spent with Alexander Langley, the Duke of Sheffield, was over. She leaned over to place a soft kiss on his lips, whispering to him as she pulled away. Her head devoid of her mask. She lay bare to him in case he would awake at that moment to see who she was. But he didn't.

"I love you, Alex."

With those last words she turned to leave. She paused at the door, her every desire to turn and beg him for whatever relationship he wanted. But she didn't. If he couldn't love her openly and honestly, then it wasn't fair to either one of them. After a while they would grow to resent each other. Not wanting that to happen, she left to cherish in her heart their time together.

Chapter Thirteen

Alex awoke to sunlight blazing into the room. When he reached for Violet, his hand encountered the cold sheets. The only thing he grabbed was her mask. It rested on the pillow next to him. He picked up the silken garment and smashed it within his grip. He sat up quickly looking for his beloved. She was gone. He knew it before his eyes searched for her. He felt it in his heart as the emptiness invaded his soul. However, he found Belle resting in the chair near the window. The look of pity in her eyes was more that he wanted to see. He rubbed his hands across his face.

"When did she leave?"

"At dawn."

He nodded. There was nothing left to say. Violet spoke it for them when she departed without saying goodbye. It was time for him to resume his life. He had a lady he needed to court for marriage. No more stolen moments. Violet would only be a memory he could reflect on when he felt lonely.

"I am surprised at your behavior, Sheffield."

"How so, Belle?" His voice held a hint of dejection.

"The old Sheffield would demand her name. He would bully me into betraying her confidence so that he could lord his title to discover what he wanted to know. This man who lies before me is a man I have never met."

"Not now, Belle. Right now, I understand her motives and I am respecting them. Later, I don't know how I will feel or what my reactions may be. For now, I must give her the freedom she deserves. She gave me the greatest gift that I shall cherish always. There can be no more, even I am aware of that. What I wanted to request of her would never have worked. She is too precious a lady to have been asked that."

"Stop, before you make me cry."

Sheffield's laugh grew bitter at her words. "I guess today is the day for all miracles."

"Weird isn't it? How one woman has impacted you to this degree?"

"Violet is a gem who shines brightly as no other."

"Yes, and she will continue to shine even more after her time spent here."

"If you don't mind, Belle, I would like to be off before I realize how deeply her loss has affected me. This room already holds too many memories that I need to run from."

Belle rose and walked to Sheffield's side. She lowered her head and placed a kiss upon his cheek. She ruffled her fingers through his hair before she left. Once the door closed, he took notice of every square inch of the bedroom. Every spot reminded him of Violet. Her smile. Her touch. The sweet scent of her. Her laughter. Her husky moans. The longer he stayed here, the more his need grew. Alongside his need, his anger flourished. With a swipe of the bed sheets he rose to pour himself a drink. After two shots of drinking the fiery liquid, his frustration was fueled more. For Violet loved to kiss the flavor of whiskey from his lips. He threw the glass into the fire, swearing his fury. He dressed to leave the memories behind. Before he left, he lifted her mask and straightened it out with fingers that shook. With a delicacy, he folded the material and placed the garment in the pocket of his suit jacket.

As Belle stood outside the bedroom, she heard Sheffield's pain. She cringed at the sound of glass breaking and knew that no matter how he hid his emotions, Violet had broken his heart. However, Belle held a few secrets. One of them involved Lady Sophia, not Violet. Now that her side of the plan was complete, it fell to Sidney to finish the rest. Soon, Sheffield would become enamored of his Violet in a different light. Belle chuckled as she walked to the parlor where her guest waited to hear how the future needed to proceed. When Sophia left this morning, it was to the same effect. Not the anger, but the sadness. Tears had slid along her cheeks and her eyes reflected the lost part of her soul.

~~~~~~

Sophia arrived at home without the servants noticing. She slipped into her bedroom and curled upon her bed in a fit of tears. They wouldn't stop streaming down her face, one after another gliding along her cheek resting in her hair. She hugged the pillow to her chest as she poured her soul into a misery she'd never held before. Walking away from Sheffield as he slept was the cowardly way to leave. But she knew if she stayed, he could persuade her with his wishes. Her tears choked her, making her sick. She needed to be quiet in case her maid overheard her despair. She'd only stopped at home to gather a bag. Then she would depart to Sidney and Wilde's house to stay with them until her parents returned. She would confess her sins to her friend. Sidney had been patient, waiting for her questions to be answered, and wouldn't judge her. Sophia held knowledge of Sidney and Rory's plot to destroy Sheffield. Now that she had given her heart to Alex, it would be up to her to dissuade them from their justice-seeking vendetta.

After a long enough time of feeling sorry for herself, she rose and discarded her gown. When she lifted her chemise over her head, her necklace became twisted in the straps. Necklace? Sophia wore no jewelry while she was with Alex. After she untangled the mess, she lifted the jewelry from her neck. She gazed at the necklace in her hand. It was a simple piece with a silver chain and locket. A locket with an amethyst jewel set into a heart. More tears slid along Sophia's cheeks at the symbolism of the gift. Alex gifted her with his heart. She choked out a sob and slid to the floor with grief. With a kiss to the jewel, she placed the necklace back around her throat and clutched the locket over her heart.

The rest of the morning Sophia sat there rocking as she tucked the memories of their time together away. She needed to move on with life. She loved a man out of her reach.

~~~~~~

Sheffield walked into his study to find that Wildeburg had made himself at home. The marquess rested in Sheffield's favorite chair and drank his best scotch. Sheffield scowled at his friend and motioned for him to move. When Wilde held up his hand, Sheffield nodded. Wilde poured him a drink and toasted him.

"You are a hard man to locate," Wilde drawled.

Sheffield lifted his eyebrow arrogantly, indicating that he didn't have to explain himself to anyone. His absence from the social scene would not go unnoticed. His grandmother had already made demands for his attendance. He was sure gossip spread among the ton. All false, but rumors, nonetheless. As long as none tied him to Violet. If any involved her, Sheffield would damage whoever spread the lies.

Wilde sighed. "I am here at the request of my bride. She wishes to invite you to our home for a dinner party. I have laid the invitation on your desk."

"I thought your wife hated me."

"She does, but she has agreed to overlook her hatred for the sake of our friendship. If you attend, it is with the order to avoid Lady Sophia. Sidney does not wish the occasion ruined by your overbearing attitude toward her friend."

During the time he spent with Violet, Sheffield had acknowledged his bad behavior. He was a brute to Lady Sophia and also to Lady Sidney. For Violet's sake, he would offer apologies to both women. She encouraged him to be a better man.

"I will apologize to your wife and to Lady Sophia. Your wife is correct with her opinion of me. I will attempt to be a more honorable duke. Please thank your wife for the invitation and give her my acceptance. I would be delighted to attend your dinner party."

Wilde sat in shock. This was not Sheffield. Who was this stranger? As he lounged across from him, he noted slight changes to his friend's demeanor. Was this a result of his time spent with Sophia as Violet? Did she hold an impact on his behavior?

"I won't question your change of attitude. Instead, I will enjoy it while it lasts."

"I owe you an apology too, Wilde. I have been an ass for most of our friendship. Especially when I realized how much you loved Sidney. I blackmailed her into accepting my marriage proposal, just so I could declare myself the victor. So, please accept my forgiveness." Sheffield rose and held out his hand to Wilde.

Wilde shook his hand, becoming more surprised. "I forgive you."

The moment turned awkward, Wilde still overwhelmed by this new behavior. Sheffield was lost in his thoughts of Violet. He wanted to be alone with his heartache. He thought about pouring his soul into drinking from his bar, but it wouldn't bring her back. It was time he entered society again.

"What function is the rage for this evening?" he asked Wilde.

"The Dancaster Soiree. Will you be attending?"

"Yes, I believe I shall. Will you and your lovely wife be in attendance?"

"Yes, and I believe Lady Sophia will be joining us."

"Perfect, I can begin to make amends."

"We shall see you tonight."

"'Til this evening, Wildeburg."

~~~~~~

Sophia settled into a suite in the Wildeburg's townhome. Sidney rested on a chaise across from her, watching as Sophia wandered around the room, not saying a word. Sophia had promised Sidney she would confide in her at the end of the week. The time had come to confess her sins.

With a heavy heart Sophia laid on the chaise too putting her head on Sidney's lap. Sidney's hand ran over her hair, comforting her. She didn't need to speak around Sidney. Their ever-lasting friendship through the years conveyed her heartache. More tears leaked, her pain consuming her. How was she to attend entertainments with Alex present and pretend they were not lovers? She must. He wouldn't be Alex anymore; he would once again be Sheffield. The duke who was a thorn in her side, making her life unbearable. Except she no longer viewed him in those terms, which brought forth a fresh batch of tears.

"Shh, Phee. It will all be well soon."

"How? My life is in ruins and my heart bleeds."

Sidney stroked Phee's hair as her crying soaked her dress. Sophia arrived at her home for a place to stay while her parents were away at their estate. They opened their door to her for as long as she needed. Belle had sent word earlier to inform her that Sophia and Sheffield's time had ended. Her friend ached, and Sidney planned everything for the oncoming week to bring her to Sheffield's attention. If she convinced Sheffield of Sophia's worth over Dallis MacPherson, then they could overcome their differences and enjoy a happily ever after.

"Your heart will heal."

"Never. I love him too deeply, there will be no other."

"Of course not, dear. I only imply there is no need for your heartache."

"You do not understand, you have Wilde."

"And you shall have Sheffield, if he is the one your heart desires. Why, I have no clue. The man is a complete ass."

"No, you don't know him as I do."

"Thank God."

Sophia rose and stood over Sidney, pointing a finger. "Do not ever speak ill of him again."

"He draws the spitfire out in you. I approve and I will grant him this."

Sophia glared at her.

"I always wondered if it simmered beneath your sweet *everybody is wonderful* persona. It is very becoming on your nature."

Sophia's glare intensified.

"But as I continue to regard you, a glow shimmers off your aura."

"What nonsense you speak."

"Do I, Phee?"

Sophia rolled her eyes as she opened the wardrobe to decide on a dress for the evening. Sidney still hadn't questioned her whereabouts for the week, or her relationship with Sheffield. Sophia sighed and turned around.

"You already know."

"Yes, I am aware of your intimacy with the duke."

"Then you realize the scandal that could be uncovered?"

"None will. Nobody but Wilde, Belle, and I hold knowledge of your arrangement."

"Too many people."

"No, only those who love you and wish for your happiness."

"Was this how you felt with Wilde? Did you feel this hopelessness suffocating your happiness?"

"Yes, when he didn't appear at the Steadhampton Musical. Then it became more painful when he never arrived to ask for my hand after we made love at Belle's."

"But he did eventually show and profess his love to you. Sheffield never will. He is clueless that I am the same person as Violet."

"Yes, Wilde did. Sheffield will soon fall at your feet too. Now, on to our plans for this evening. I have asked Rory to be your escort for the Dancaster Soiree."

Sophia nodded. Sweet Rory, he would cheer her spirits. Also, she needed to apologize for her fit of anger the last time they met.

"Do you love him?"

"Yes."

"Do you want to fight for him?"

"Yes."

"I hoped so."

"Sidney, please tell me you haven't planned anything?"

"Perhaps a bit of an experiment. Only if you are game."

"I thought you wanted to destroy him?"

"That was before my best friend fell hopelessly in love with him."

"Can I ask what your plans are?"

"I think it would be best if you were innocent of any elements that I've made to bring your courtship to par."

"Sidney?"

"Trust me, my dear. Everything will go smoothly, for I have planned to the last detail."

"That is what I am afraid of."

"No need to worry. Now, what do you plan to wear this evening?"

Sophia knew she should question Sidney further on her meddling, but her friend would not utter a word of her plans. Her life was in Sidney's hands now. She trusted Sidney with her happiness. It couldn't go too horribly wrong. Sidney had landed a marquess and fallen madly in love. Maybe Sidney could bring Sheffield around to notice her charms, not Violet's? Her fingers clutched the pendant hanging from her neck, praying she was right.

Chapter Fourteen

Sheffield stood against the pillar as he watched the ton scrutinize him from under their eyelashes. His presence tonight caused quite a stir. He heard the whispered gossip floating in the air around him. He regarded his peers in a different light. Violet spoke of them during their time together. She explained the reasons why they behaved as they did. She described the wallflowers to him, the drunken rogues, the lonely widows, and also the shameful brides. As he watched the people mingling, he saw them through her eyes. Her sweet and gentle nature never spoke a bad word against a soul.

He glanced over to the wallflowers and decided to offer one of the young ladies a dance. His next conquest sat in a chair beside her grandmother, Lady Ratcliff. Sheffield approached them, asking for a dance on her card. The chit glared her hatred at him. However, she couldn't deny him, for if she gave him the cut direct, it would ruin her season. No gentleman would ever court her. She passed him her card, where he signed for the first dance of the evening, a waltz. Excellent, he could spend the dance repairing the damage of his overbearing attitude from the past few weeks. He would apologize, then proceed to invite her for a ride in the park tomorrow. He offered a few kind words to Lady Ratcliff hoping to charm his way into a courtship. After he secured his dance, he wandered onto the balcony.

Sophia watched him from afar. When Sheffield asked Lady Dallis for a dance, her heart tore a little more. She didn't know if she could bear to watch the beauty dancing in the arms of the man she loved. She wanted to follow him outside. After her first step, a hand gripped her arm, halting her. Sidney softly restrained her with a shake of her head. Sidney was correct. Sophia stopped and sighed.

"Trust me," Sidney whispered.

Her trust lay in an idea that would only end in disaster, but it was Sophia's only option. She decided as she dressed for this evening that she would fight for him. Sheffield didn't know who she was, but she wanted him to love Sophia as well as Violet. For him to love Sophia, he must see her for who she was. If she won him as Violet, then she could conquer him as Sophia. She turned her head and flashed Sidney a wavering smile as she squeezed the hand lying on her arm.

Soon, Sheffield re-entered the ballroom and saw Wilde and his bride standing with a small group of people. Within their circle were Lady Sophia and Lord Rory Beckwith. He scowled as the earl stood close to Lady Sophia, whispering in her ear. When her face lighted with laughter and her hand playfully slapped him on the arm, Sheffield was overcome with jealousy. Why would he be possessive over her? She was an opinionated chit who always angered him. It must be the long blonde hair, for it reminded him of Violet. His footsteps led him closer, stopping near. He didn't understand why he was drawn to Sophia.

Rory noticed Sheffield's nearness to Sophia, and he moved closer. His protectiveness was for a reason. He was aware of the duke's fascination with Sophia and disagreed with his actions. He couldn't defend her honor, but he could prevent it from happening again. Sophia trembled underneath his touch, and her eyes darted to the duke. A blush spread over her face as Sheffield's stare became noticeable to everybody in the small group. Rory heard Wilde clear his throat. Still Sheffield wouldn't break his stare from Sophia. Anger consumed Rory, and he wanted to call the duke out. He stepped forward, but Sidney stopped him too.

Sidney wondered if she was to restrain everybody this evening. Why didn't the subjects in this experiment follow the guidelines of proper etiquette? What made this worse was that she acted more proper than everybody else. Whereas before Sidney's two friends usually had to correct her. Now she held them back from causing a scene. Thankfully, her husband read the message she silently sent and intervened.

"Sheffield, how are you this fine evening?"

Sheffield drew his gaze away from Lady Sophia. "Very well, Wilde. May I say how enchanting you ladies are?"

Sophia blushed at his comment and spoke softly. "Thank you, Your Grace."

"Ahh, now he displays the charm," Sidney teased.

Sheffield laughed at her joke as it broke the tension. "If I may be so bold as to request a dance from both of you lovely ladies."

"Sorry old chap, my wife's dance card is full." Wilde said, wrapping his arm around Sidney's waist, drawing her to his side.

"Of course, how indecent of me to ask a new bride. Lady Sophia, do you have a dance open to share with me?"

Everybody knew she must answer yes; she fell in the same trap as Lady Dallis if she refused. "I do." She handed him her dance card.

Sheffield signed his name and then made his excuses as he wandered to mingle with the other guests. He would make his apologies during their dance. He'd requested the second waltz of the ball. It would appear the waltzes of the evening would be full of requests for forgiveness. He hoped both women would excuse his boorish behavior from the start of the season. As he walked the room, his gaze kept straying to Lady Sophia.

Her poise and open personality drew every member of the ton to their circle. Her smile would light up the atmosphere. He followed none of the conversations flowing around him, because she caught his attention. Sheffield excused himself and leaned against the wall, nursing his drink as he stared at her.

His eyes devoured her. She lifted her head and their gazes met. Her look devoured him. For endless moments they were lost in each other. What color were her eyes? Violet? He was dismayed at what he was doing—how could he forget Violet so easily for another? The ladies shared similarities, nothing more. Violet held his heart, didn't she? Before he pulled his gaze away, he glimpsed at the hurt in her eyes. When he glanced back, she continued to stare at him. He smiled and lifted his drink. She sent him a smile filled with sadness. Soon the conversation was flowing around Sophia again.

The orchestra played a few notes, drawing the dancers to the ballroom floor. He rested his drink on a platter a servant carried. He approached Lady Dallis and escorted her onto the dance floor. Sheffield also saw Beckwith leading Lady Sophia through the steps. He needed to focus on the woman in his arms, she was his only hope for the future. He required Lady Dallis to help ease the scandal of his family document. If he couldn't charm her into becoming his duchess, then the Sheffield line would be in disgrace. With one last glance at the possessiveness of Beckwith's hold, and the smooth glide of Lady Sophia's body as she moved to the music, he turned his focus toward Lady Dallis.

"Thank you for agreeing to dance with me." He attempted civility with the chit.

"Well, your rank guaranteed that I would respond with a yes."

He sensed her hatred, so he tried again. "I would like to offer my apologies for my boorish behavior toward you from earlier in the season. I understand I came off strong and assumed you would fall at my feet in gratitude. It has come to my attention how disrespectful it was of me to treat you in that nature."

Dallis didn't want to dance with the duke. His conceited attitude during the previous occasions they'd met infuriated her to no ends. When she gave him a put-down at the last ball, her odds of finding a husband this season ended. But when the duke disappeared from social functions for over a week and nobody turned their back on Dallis or her grandmother, she considered herself safe. When he requested a dance this evening, Dallis became on guard waiting for their dance. At any moment Sheffield could embarrass her.

When he started talking again, she lost her concentration. Her gaze caught Lord Rory Beckwith dancing with the known beauty of the ton, Lady Sophia Turlington. She had not met the blonde, but everybody spoke of how her loveliness was not only on the outside, but it filled her soul. Never a mean word passed from her lips about another person. They say she would find something special about everyone and make them believe in it too. Her eyes had stayed glued on the couple once they walked into the soiree together with Lord and Lady Wildeburg. The earl never left Lady Sophia's side. When Sheffield approached their group, Lord Beckwith became possessive over Sophia. Were they a couple? No gossip spread of him courting her. Was she mistaken? Disappointment settled as Dallis viewed their familiarity with each other and he swept Sophia across the dance floor. Dallis thought she'd grabbed the earl's eye at the Caulfield Ball, when he rescued her from Sheffield. But he'd never paid a visit to her grandmother's or asked for a dance since then. She sighed. When Sheffield swung her in a circle, Dallis lost view of them. She returned her attention to Sheffield. He was in the middle of explaining his past actions and apologizing for his indecent behavior. What?

"I am sorry, Your Grace. What were you saying?"

"I am offering my sincere apology for assuming you should be grateful for my regard. It was wrong of me to be so callous."

Dallis searched his gaze, listening to his wholehearted words, and saw his sincerity. Her stare took in the sadness lurking in his depths. Something had recently happened to cause him this despair.

"Thank you for your apology, Your Grace."

"If I may continue to be so bold. Can I escort you with a ride through the park on the morrow?"

"I have a fear of horses, but we can walk if that is agreeable with you."

"Yes, that is agreeable with me."

The waltz ended with Sheffield returning her to Lady Ratcliff and the promise of seeing her tomorrow for their outing. His eyes searched for Lady Sophia again. He couldn't find her, but he did see Beckwith walking inside alone. They had been dancing. Was she now on the terrace? If so, this was the perfect moment to offer his apology instead of when they danced. He didn't understand why, but when they were to dance, he only wanted to hold her and not to grovel at her feet.

Sophia rested against the balustrade, the necklace clutched in her hand. She sensed Sheffield's regard the entire evening. Had he guessed her identity? She couldn't wear the locket, so she kept the jewelry hidden inside her reticule. When Rory left to fetch them a drink, Sophia assured him she would be safe. She pointed out how Lady Dallis occupied Sheffield's attention, which only deepened his scowl. Did Rory continue to harbor an attachment toward Lady Dallis? If so, it would explain the reason for his hostility toward Sheffield. She would question him when he returned.

"A lovely evening to enjoy the stars." A voice spoke from behind, startling her.

She gasped as she spun around. Sheffield stood silhouetted in the moonlight. The dark enhancing his powerful stature. Her eyes devoured him as if she had not seen him in ages, when only this morning she'd left his side. He dressed simple this evening, with a dark suit and red cravat and vest. She wished to smooth her hand across his jacket and straighten his tie, but knew such an intimate action would arouse his curiosity. She gripped her hands tighter to prevent herself from reaching out, and remembered she held the locket. Hurriedly she shoved the necklace into her reticule, only to drop it on the ground. She knelt to gather it, and their hands met.

He didn't mean to frighten her; he only wished to apologize. When she turned at his comment, her eyes grew large in what Sheffield perceived to be fear. It was then he understood his past actions regarding Sophia would haunt him. The disappointment surprised him. Sheffield aspired to live his life in a way to make Violet proud. To achieve that, he must offer amends to Lady Sophia. For whatever reason, this woman rubbed him wrong. They always sparked when they were near each other. Most of her dislike came from comments he'd made toward Lady Sidney when he'd courted her. The rest were by his actions. Two times he kissed her with no regard to her reputation. For that he was sorry. He didn't even remember the kisses, only that he took them in anger. He should never treat any lady in that degree.

Sheffield saw Sophia place an object inside her reticule, before the bag slipped from her fingers. He knelt to retrieve the purse. Their hands met, and he heard the sharp intake of her breath. Her hands were small, and her touch gentle. He wished to caress her more, but their gloves prevented him from feeling how soft her skin would be. His thumb brushed across her knuckles before she withdrew from his grasp. She rose from him and took a few steps backward. He followed, holding her reticule. His eyes met Sophia's and became lost in her soulful gaze. Once again, he wondered at the color, only for the dark night to deny his wish. He secretly wished them to be violet. Was he so desperate for Violet that he even wished the one lady he couldn't get along with to be her?

He was too close. Sophia needed to leave before she poured out her heart. His kindness was her undoing. Why did he treat her differently this evening? She could handle this situation better if he was Sheffield. The overbearing, egotistical, arrogant, Duke of Sheffield. No, instead he behaved as Alex. Her heart ached as she felt the need to vanish. He handed her the reticule with the chain from her necklace hanging out. He attempted to untangle the chain and she grabbed it from him, afraid that he would see his gift. He stepped away and dropped his hands.

"I am sorry."

"No, it is my fault. I am the one who dropped my reticule."

"No, that is not the reason I seek your forgiveness."

Lady Sophia looked upon him in confusion. Her lips pursed into a cute bow. When she brought her teeth out to bite her bottom lip, as she tried to figure out the reason he needed to apologize, he felt a stirring of desire. He craved to slide his tongue along and sooth her bruised mouth. Then he wanted to explore the sweet taste. He remembered kissing her, and the memories of her innocence as he ravaged her. She never pushed him away but kissed him in return. Would she let him kiss her again? His body behaved with a mind of his own as he took a step closer to feel her heat. When she didn't retreat, he lifted his hand to brush a curl lying across her cheek. He still couldn't see the color of her eyes, but he noticed that they darkened at his touch.

"What are you sorry for, Sheffield?" she whispered.

Alex consumed her. She needed Sheffield to show his true colors before she melted at his feet. As much as she would regret this, Sophia pulled the curl out of his grasp and moved away. She walked farther along the terrace, closer to the doors.

Sheffield stared as she walked away. He closed his eyes, forcing himself to forget her. Lady Sophia was not Violet. Trying to turn her into Violet in his mind would not solve his need to move on with life. He'd come tonight intending to right his wrongs. Touching Sophia and wishing to kiss her again would not bring Violet back.

"If you would allow me to explain."

Lady Sophia nodded, waiting for him to declare his intentions.

"This past week, someone has brought to my attention my rude behavior. Upon reflection, I now understand how my actions have caused you distress. So, for that I want to beg your forgiveness and I promise never to behave in that manner again."

"Might I inquire as to why your change of attitude?"

"A very special woman came into my life recently and impacted me greatly. Through her vision I have re-evaluated how I live and treat people. It pains me to admit that I have been a bore. I want to do justice to the short time we spent together and hope to make her proud."

Sophia drowned in his words. Tears rushed at his honest confession. She wanted to shout to him that she was proud.

"This woman is special to you?"

"Yes, more than she ever understood."

"I will admit, she has changed you. Your new behavior has made an impression. It will be interesting to watch what other differences she makes in your life."

"Sadly to say, none."

"Thrown her over already?"

"No, she left."

Why she kept asking him questions was beyond her. Sophia knew the answers. Ego? Did she want to hear him praise her more? Or did she not wish to leave him? The sadness in Sheffield's voice matched that in Sophia's heart. She needed to return to the ballroom, she could no longer play him false.

"I am sorry for your loss. I accept your apology, Sheffield."

"Thank you."

Sophia smiled sorrowfully as she turned to enter the ballroom. Before she took a step, Rory stormed through the door. The fierceness of his gaze as he saw Sheffield fueled his anger. He advanced on Sheffield and slugged him across the jaw. Sheffield, unaware of any coming assault, didn't have time to react and stumbled backward. However, Rory wasn't finished with his fists. He punched Sheffield in the gut, causing him to double over in pain. Rory threw more punches, each one with more force. With a final punch to his head, Sheffield toppled over and passed out.

Chapter Fifteen

Now Rory wanted to be the hero when it wasn't necessary. Sheffield was apologizing to her, not harassing her. Sophia glanced around to see if anyone noticed the attack. Nobody was in sight, and the music coming from the door indicated a dance was in progress. They only had a small amount of time for Rory to move Sheffield before the terrace filled. She must not have any scandal involving her with Sheffield. Her parents would insist on marriage and then he would know the full length of her deceit. He would blame her for trapping him. No, she would win his heart and then confess, not this way.

"You idiot. Now you come to my defense?"

"I told you never to be alone with him again."

Sophia whispered her argument so not to draw attention. "Once again, you left me alone. Also, you are not my keeper, Rory Beckwith. The gentleman apologized for his past behavior. Now look at what you have done. A fine mess you have caused."

Rory winced. "Damn."

"That one word does not even begin to describe this. I will fetch Wilde to assist you. Pull his body deeper into the shadows, I will return soon."

Damn. Damn. Damn. As he watched Sophia enter the ballroom, Rory admitted this was more than a fine mess. It was a catastrophe. The repercussions of his actions would settle upon them in tidal waves. His family taking the brunt of his stupidity. When he'd returned to the terrace and Sheffield was near Sophia, all he saw was red. Not only had he just watched the man hold the woman of his dreams in a dance, he was now accosting sweet Sophia again. The previous two times Rory did nothing in her honor. This time he wouldn't fail her. She deserved better from him. Sophia gave him the gift of friendship and in return Rory gave her cowardice. Not this time. His anger was already brewing below the surface. It was men like Sheffield who made people's lives miserable if they so choose. Sheffield took what he wanted and discarded what he no longer needed. At this moment, Sheffield wanted Lady Dallis MacPherson and she was powerless to deny him. Rory wanted her too. His foot struck out to kick Sheffield in his side. A moan echoed from the body.

"Rory Beckwith, shame on you," Sophia hissed. "The man is down and yet you continue to abuse him."

Rory cringed as not only Sophia but also Sidney and Wildeburg caught his actions. Sidney kept shaking her head at him, shooting him with a look of *stupid, stupid, stupid.* She ordered Rory to be on his best behavior and keep his temper under control. She told him the future had a way of working itself out. He was furious with her for backing out on their plan to destroy Sheffield. Sidney had explained a conflict of interest had arose and she needed to rethink her plan. Now, here he was branded the villain, and they directed their sympathy toward Sheffield. Why did evil always win? From this moment forward, he would take what he desired and damn whoever stood in his way. He didn't need Sidney to find the document. He had a clue where Lord Hartridge hid his research. He would take it upon himself to destroy Sheffield and win Lady Dallis's heart. For now, he would help them clean the mess he created. After that, they were on their own.

Tomorrow he would apologize to Sophia, for he was at fault toward her, but to nobody else.

"I have instructed my carriage to the back of the garden. Help me carry him, Beckwith." Wilde said.

"Why don't you throw him in his own carriage like the scum he is?" Rory shot back.

"His carriage is to remain here to deliver his grandmother home. I have already delivered a message to her from Sheffield. I explained how an issue with Parliament called him away, and he left the carriage for a safe ride home. Now hurry, before the musicians finish the set and someone sees us."

The two men carried Sheffield into the waiting carriage. After helping the women inside, Wilde turned to Rory. He had no advice to offer the man, his feelings torn. He couldn't defend Sheffield's actions toward Sophia without giving her secret away. He understood Rory's frustrations, for he'd felt this way toward Sheffield not so long ago. Somehow, he would need to steer Rory away from Sophia. Sheffield already stole her heart. Perhaps Sidney could draw his interest toward another lady. With a shake of his head, he entered the carriage. As he moved to sit in the seat with Sheffield, he paused seeing Sophia in his seat with Sheffield's head lying in her lap. She caressed the bruises along his jaw. She had removed her gloves so her fingertips lightly grazed his face. Wilde's gaze shot to Sidney and she shrugged at him. He sighed and moved to the bench beside Sidney before Rory noticed the scene. The poor man had suffered enough tonight without having to witness Sophia displaying her affections toward another man.

"You are playing a dangerous game, my friend. What if he should awaken?" Wilde warned Sophia.

"Then I will only explain how I tended to his wounds."

"You're not afraid he will make the connection between you and Violet?"

Sophia's gaze rose to Wilde then shifted to Sidney. The message she sent her friend was clear. It was the look of betrayal.

"He figured the deception before you told me, Phee. It appears Sheffield was into his cups about a chit named Violet who worked at Belle's. The description was too familiar to Wilde, so he approached Belle. We both kept your secret for the sake of love. Please do not be angry with Wilde or myself. We only have your best interest at heart."

Sophia sighed. For her feeling of betrayal was silly. She was the one at fault in this entire mess. Her deceit had spiraled out of control and her secrets were not for them to bear. Her fingers brushed through Sheffield's hair.

"Violet," he murmured as his eyelids fluttered open.

Sophia froze, drawing her hand away. "No, 'tis I, Lady Sophia."

Sheffield groaned as he felt the sting in his jaw. "What the bloody hell happened?"

"I fear you took a beating."

"Did I deserve it?" He gazed into her concerned eyes.

Sheffield stared as she shook her head no. The hurt in her glance mesmerized him. He felt as if she ached for him. That his injuries were hers. Which was nonsense. Still, the color eluded him, but the touch of her fingers as they caressed his hair did not. It reminded him of Violet. Lady Sophia was as gentle and caring as his lost love.

Sophia became trapped in his gaze with nowhere to run and hide. His hand found hers and brought her fingers to his lips. He kissed them softly as he continued to stare into her eyes. Both became lost and oblivious to the other occupants of the carriage. He turned her hand over and placed a kiss in her palm.

"Violet," he sighed.

"You must have got knocked harder than we realized, my good man." Wilde said.

The carriage stopped, bringing a halt to their affections. Wilde punched Sheffield on the shoulder, breaking their stare. Sheffield wondered, how was it he never noticed how exquisite Lady Sophia was? Her grace calmed him as he began to remember how he came to be in this predicament. Lady Sophia had accepted his apology, before Lord Beckwith slammed his fist into his face. After a few more punches, Beckwith knocked him senseless. He would be angry with the earl later, but for now he was lost in the charms of Violet. He closed his eyes and opened them again. No, Lady Sophia.

"You are in pain." Her soft voice soothed him.

Now she even sounded like her. He needed to leave the carriage before he made a fool of himself. Which, he was sure, Wilde and even Sidney would appreciate. However, he didn't want to send the wrong message to Lady Sophia and cause her any more discomfort. He sat forward and felt more aches upon his body. He opened the door and stepped from the carriage. Sheffield's knees buckled as he hit the ground. Wilde leapt out and with the help of a footman guided him inside his townhome. Sheffield regretted not answering her, but his injured state caused him embarrassment.

Wilde returned and informed the driver to see the ladies home and return within an hour. He opened the carriage and reassured Sophia over Sheffield's condition. He would see to Sheffield's injuries and would inform them of his condition when he returned home. After the ladies departed, he entered Sheffield's townhome and searched for his friend, finding him already drinking from a new bottle of whiskey and staring into the fire.

Wilde might be longer than an hour. His friend looked more depressed than he had ever seen before.

"This is becoming a habit, Sheffield."

"Bugger off."

"What happened on the terrace?"

"Your wife's friend slugged me then proceeded to beat the living hell out me."

"Why?"

"How the hell should I know? One minute I was apologizing to Lady Sophia, the next I'm riding passed out in your carriage with my head on her lap."

"Did you force yourself on her?"

His bitter laugh echoed around him. How ironic, Wilde accused him of the very thing he asked forgiveness for. Sheffield supposed he deserved the beating for his past indiscretions. Now as he sat here getting drunk, they seemed irredeemable. How could he have treated Lady Sophia so callously? After having spent time in her company, he now understood her charm.

"No, I only asked for her forgiveness. She granted it and was returning to the ballroom, when Beckwith's fist connected with my face."

He reached to rub his jaw. He flinched at the pain, but his mind tried to place a memory. Lady Sophia caressing his face as she soothed him. He tried remembering the conversation he'd heard as he came to light. He could only recall Wilde mentioning a game with Lady Sophia. The more he tried to remember, the more his head ached. He pinched the bridge of his nose and lowered his eyes, leaning his head against the chair.

"Getting drunk is not the best medicine for the beating you took."

"Please send my deep regrets to your wife and Lady Sophia. I will call tomorrow to visit with Sidney and pay a visit to Lord Turlington to speak with Lady Sophia."

"No need, Lady Sophia is staying at our home until her parents return from their estate."

He opened his eyes and sat forward. "Her parents are away?"

"Yes, they should return home soon."

"How long have they been away?"

"Since this morning. That is when she came to stay with us."

Sheffield slumped in his chair, disappointed. Violet's parents were supposedly away at their estate too—it gave her the freedom to be with him for the week. Still, the similarities between the two women confused him. Was Lady Sophia his Violet? If so, it would explain hiding her identity. If he had known, he would not have pursued her. However, now that Violet stole his heart and Sophia might be her; how could he not pursue her?

"Then her parents have only just left this morning?"

"Yes."

"Then I shall kill two birds with one stone and visit both ladies tomorrow."

"Sheffield, I think it would be best for you to stay away. After tonight, you have caused too many scenes with Lady Sophia. Soon, rumors will spread, and the ton will have you married in a fortnight."

Wilde watched as Sheffield kept drinking from the bottle. Something besides Violet troubled his friend.

"Talk, Sheffield."

"Talk about what, my friend? How you stole my one chance at happiness? She was to be my redemption for the past sins of my family."

"How so?"

"A scandal will unfold once Lord Hartridge's research is complete. I needed to secure myself a duchess of the highest standings before someone exposes the information."

"How was Sidney of the highest standing? Her family holds no resources of power."

"You are correct. However, the Crown values her father. I wouldn't be scorned with her family's influence. Now I am forced to search for another duchess whose family will back me in the face of a scandal. Lady Dallis is my only option available."

"Then explain your anger toward Lady Sophia."

"She kept me from winning Sidney's heart. She encouraged your pursuit. It angered me. Also, there is a spark when I am around her that sets me on edge. This evening we seemed to have reached an unspoken agreement to put the past behind us, before Beckwith landed a planter on my face."

"Is that also the reason why you never pursued Lady Sophia?"

"Her father is the person responsible for disclosing the secret paper that will destroy me. If Lord Hartridge finds any truth to the document, Lord Turlington will strip me of my power in Parliament, and take my title and lands. I suppose that is part of the reason why I have shown only disrespect toward Lady Sophia."

"Who else knows?"

"Nobody else. I trust Lord Hartridge to keep this to himself. Even with his anger at my treatment of his daughter, he will not reveal my secret."

"I think until you learn the truth, you need to keep your distance from Lady Sophia. I will pass your sentiments to her and my wife. Continue your pursuit with Lady Dallis, although I fear you will not come to a marriage contract with her either."

"Why not?"

Wilde laughed. "When she looks at you it is with hatred."

"I am taking her for a walk in the park tomorrow."

"Good luck, my friend."

"Go home to your bride, Wilde."

Wilde chuckled as he left Sheffield to his bottle of whiskey. He'd warned him away, hoping it would be the draw for him seeking Sophia's attention. Now, he needed to arrange for Sophia to be at the park tomorrow at the same time as Sheffield and Lady Dallis. He thought of the perfect gentleman for the job. He whistled a tune as he walked to the carriage. When he climbed inside, excited to return home to his wife, she surprised him by being there in the cab, waiting for him and wearing his coat with nothing underneath.

"You took long enough, Lord Wildeburg."

"I was only helping your research project along, Lady Wildeburg."

"Mmm," she murmured against his lips as the carriage took them for a ride.

Chapter Sixteen

Sidney persuaded Sophia to allow Rory to accompany her for a walk through the park. When he arrived to apologize for his behavior the previous evening, Sophia refused to see him. With gentle encouragement from Sidney she relented. She was too soft. Sophia knew in her heart, there was a deeper reason for Rory's anger toward Sheffield than defending her honor. Sophia didn't like the rift in their friendship and if he was a gentleman enough to fix the problem, then she could listen to him.

Also, taking a walk with Rory was preferable to moping in her room for a man out of her reach. Even after Wilde assured her this morning that Sheffield's condition was no worse for wear and the beating probably did him good, Sophia still held concern for his welfare. Rory was known for his fighting; his hands were brutal from the boxing matches he engaged in for fun. Well, not fun, Sophia suspected they were more for earning a dime. His family's coffers were empty, and he earned money on the side in the underground world to support his mother and sister. The ton forbade talk of such things, however Sidney kept Sophia informed of the seedier side of society. Sidney's parents were big supporters of the underprivileged and fought for equality. Sophia's parents were too upper-crust to meddle with the unfortunate. It was surprising their mothers were best friends. The two women were complete opposites.

They were silent as they walked. Each step took them closer to the pond and further away in their own thoughts. As they settled on the bench, they watched the ducks waddle out of the water. Sophia wished she'd remembered to bring some bread. A bag landed in her lap. She glanced toward Rory, who shrugged and attempted a grin.

"Did you think I would forget?"

Sophia smiled her reply as she ripped the bag open, tossing the crumbs toward the ducks. Before long, the birds attacked them quacking for their share. Sophia's mood lifted, her heart feeling lighter. She threw more pieces at the ducks that weren't getting any, laughing as they followed the trail. When her bag was empty, she laid her head on Rory's shoulders, accepting his apology with her unspoken forgiveness. He wrapped his arm around her and relaxed against the bench. There were no visitors in the park, so the closeness of their bodies went unnoticed. It was a private garden near the Wildeburg's and only the nearby residences had access.

She lifted Rory's hand into her lap, her fingers trailing across the open wounds, touching gently. These were the same hands that struck the man she loved. Each man held a special place in her heart. One of love, the other of friendship. Her feelings were torn between the two gentlemen. One she could be with, the other never to be again unless she revealed her secret.

"Do they hurt?"

"Nah."

"Why?"

"I saw red. My frustration had already reached a boiling point when he danced with Lady Dallis. I understood why she had to dance with him. It was her reaction to him that spurred my agitation."

"How did she react?"

"At first, I could tell she held him in contempt. By the time the dance concluded she regarded him in a different light. They were smiling and even laughing. Plainly, she forgave him."

"They were laughing?"

"Yes, her face was alight with smiles. Even a blush graced her cheeks. Then I overheard her grandmother telling my mother the duke had asked Dallis for a walk today."

"A walk?" Sophia kept repeating questions he'd already answered.

"It is hopeless."

"Do you care for her?"

"Do you believe in love at first sight?"

Sophia smiled, raising her head to look at him. "Yes."

"Would you believe me, if I told you the first time that I noticed Dallis across the ballroom floor, my heart stopped? Then once it started beating again, it was a different rhythm than before. Every time I see her it reacts that way."

Sophia held joy for Rory. She knew exactly what he explained, for that was how Alex made her feel. She couldn't explain any of this to him, but she encouraged him to pursue Dallis. An idea began to form that would require Sidney's help—which was right up her friend's alley. It would seem another love experiment would be in play. Only this time it would be aimed at Rory. It could intermingle with the plan involved for Sheffield and her. It was perfect.

"Never fear, my friend. You shall have your heart's desire. I only ask for you to display some patience and keep your fists held to your side. Can you control your anger?"

Rory sighed. Controlling his anger had always been an issue. He was usually one to punch first, and then ask questions later. Last night held proof of that. But for the sake of his friendship with Sophia he would try.

Also, he already promised Sidney he would. Or else he wouldn't be allowed to visit them.

"For you I will."

"Excellent, I shall have Sidney add Lady Dallis and her grandmother to her guest list for her dinner party."

"Do you think she will come?"

"Yes. Sidney and I shall pay a visit to her and Lady Ratcliff to welcome her to society and offer our friendship."

"You would do this after I have been such a terrible friend?"

"Yes, Rory. I must warn you though, Sidney invited Sheffield too, and he has accepted."

"I figured as much, since Wildeburg and he are close friends."

"Walk me back to Sidney's. We have much to accomplish."

Rory chuckled as he rose and offered Phee his arm. His mood lighter after their time together. Sophia always had the knack of making somebody feel happier. Any man who won her heart would be a lucky bastard.

When they started to walk away, they noticed they weren't alone in the park. Another couple rested on a bench near the gazebo. Not just anybody, but the two people who were never far from their thoughts. Alexander Langley and Lady Dallis. Sophia squeezed Rory's arm in a warning. Instead of speaking to them, they nodded their acknowledgements and strolled out of the gates. Neither one of them thought of the close affection they'd displayed earlier.

However, the other two sat wondering with conflicted emotions.

~~~~~

Sheffield wanted to rise the minute he saw them. With Beckwith, he wanted to gift him with the same bruises he sported. With Lady Sophia he … hell, he didn't know what he wanted. Throughout the evening his dreams consumed him, waking him in a cold sweat. Her tender touch invoked images of Violet making love with him, only when Sheffield lifted her mask it was Lady Sophia. As he'd watched them share an affectionate embrace, jealousy stirred in his gut.

"Is Lord Rory Beckwith courting Lady Sophia Turlington?" Lady Dallis asked.

"Not that I am aware of. They are close friends."

"Mmm, their intimate actions display more than friendship."

"Perhaps you are correct."

The thought didn't sit well with him, if it were the truth. Nonetheless, she was not his, nor did he hold any interest in Sophia other than as an acquaintance. He was here to pursue a courtship with Lady Dallis which would lead her to becoming his duchess. Sheffield turned his attention to his companion. She stared at him with her eyes narrowing, taking in the bruises covering his face.

"What happened to your face?"

"I was set upon by thieves."

She arched her eyebrow. "Did the so-called thieves steal your prized possession?"

Her double innuendo didn't go unnoticed. "The prized possession was never mine to begin with. I only admired it."

"Enough to own it?"

"No."

"Why not?"

"It does not hold my interest as much as you do."

"Bollocks," she muttered under her breath.

"I will pretend to ignore your vulgar language."

"If ye mean to court me, ye will need to get used to it." Dallis emphasized her Scottish brogue to offend him.

"You will allow me to court you?"

"My grandmother insists."

"And your desire?"

"It does not matter anymore after this morning."

"May I inquire as to why?"

"I guess it would not hurt to inform you. My heart lay with another, but from what my eyes can tell, he has already been taken."

Sheffield laughed at the irony of his situation. Once again, he courted a lady who loved another. Did he want to continue to pursue Dallis? It would only lead to him losing another bride. If so, no father would allow him to court their daughters, a duke or not. He would have shown an inability to keep a bride. Once would be overlooked, twice would make him a fool among the ton.

No, as much as it pained him, he would not court Lady Dallis further.

"Rory Beckwith?"

"'Tis afraid so."

"I can understand the feeling of lost love. I myself have recently suffered. However, you should not give up hope so easily."

"But I thought ..."

"I relinquish my courtship."

Lady Dallis scrutinized the Duke of Sheffield as he released her from his pursuit. Why? She decided to dig deeper. Her nanna said she was always too curious for her own good.

"Are ye bruises from Lord Beckwith?"

"Yes."

"Was Lady Sophia who you admired?"

"Yes."

"Do you love her?"

"Nay, I love another. Lady Sophia reminds me of her."

"If you love another, then why are you courting me?"

"Because I don't know her true identity."

"I am confused."

"It is a long story."

"Then as your newfound friend, perhaps you would like to share your long story."

"It is a highly improper story and very personal."

"I understand. What is her name?"

"I call her Violet."

"Why?"

"Because she has the most unusual shade of purple for an eye color."

"Now I am really intrigued."

Sheffield laughed. "Friends?"

"Friends."

"Then as your friend I must return you home before the rain falls upon our heads."

Dallis looked up and saw the impending rain clouds. He walked her back and even came inside for tea with her grandmother. He could be a very charming gentleman when he chose to be. Whoever Violet was, she was a fool.

Chapter Seventeen

Dear Lady Sophia,

    I wished to convey my regrets on the conclusion to the previous evening events. Wildeburg has suggested that I refrain from visiting, due to your delicate nature toward violence. Thank you for your tender care while I was knocked unconscious. Your gentle touch held the cure to my recovery.

    I hope you enjoyed your walk in the park with Lord Beckwith. I would have approached but did not want to subject Lady Dallis or you to the horror of my interaction toward your companion.

    I wish you well. Until the next time we meet, and may it be uneventful.

    Alexander Langley
    Duke of Sheffield

~~~

Dear Sheffield,

    It warms my heart on your speedy recovery. I have worried your injuries wear painful. 'Tis not your fault on how the Dancaster Soiree ended. Only one man ruined the entire evening. There are times that I am ashamed to call him my friend.

I too hoped your walk with Lady Dallis was pleasurable. I did not mean to be discourteous, but only wished to prevent another altercation. Lady Dallis is a lovely girl. I wish you luck in your courtship.

As for my delicate nature toward violence, all I can say is posh. While I do not condone violence of any kind, the fault did not lie with you. Please do not listen to Lord Wildeburg. I feel your past engagement to Sidney brings out the jealousy in him.

Uneventful? That is no fun.

Your new friend,
Sophia Turlington

~~~

Dear Sophia,
Are we friends?
Sheffield

~~~

Dear Sheffield,
Yes, we are. In fact, call me Phee, all my friends do.
Phee

~~~

Dear ~~Phee~~ Sophia,
Sorry, my friend. I cannot ruin the beauty of your name in that form. To me you will only be Sophia.

Sadly, Lady Dallis is in love with somebody else. I won't subject her to my courting. Why does every lady I court love another? The worst luck follows me as I try to find a bride. While I do not care for the gentleman; I wish her well. I wish you the same luck with Lord Beckwith. I only say that, because I watched your close affections with each other at the park.

Your Friend,
Alex

~~~

Dear Alex,

I hope I can call you Alex while we correspond. You signed your last letter with your name, so I assumed I could. If not, please correct me.

I am sorry to hear of your loss in courting Lady Dallis. If I may be so bold to ask, have you found your next lady to court? You are mistaken, Rory and I are only friends, his heart lies with another. I guess you could say we are two lost souls.

Do you believe in love?

Your Friend
Phee

~~~

Dear Sophia,

You are Sophia to me, not Phee. Sign your letters accordingly.

Love? A heavy word. Do friends discuss such intimate subjects? I find this highly unorthodox, but I feel a trust with you that I don't share with others. So, to answer your question, yes, love is real. I am in love now, but I fear I have lost her. I never declared my affections to her. Now, I suffer regret on letting her walk out of my life.

Do you hold the same faith in love?

Alex

~~~

Dear ~~Alex,~~ Alexander

I prefer Alexander to Alex. <u>Please,</u> sign your letters accordingly. (Do you see how I requested, not demanded?)

I trust you too. Yes, I believe in love. For I gave my heart to a man who holds no clue I even exist. I sense he loves me too, but not who I truly am.

You should find your true love and never let her go.

Yours Sophia

~~~

Dear Sophia,

I am forever apologizing to you. Please forgive me once again for being demanding. You may sign your letters however you wish.

I have taken your advice and sent a request asking for permission to visit with her. Wish me luck.

I also have a desire to call on you. Perhaps, I can accompany you on a walk tomorrow in the park. That is if Wildeburg will allow it.

A man hoping you will agree.

Alexander

P.S. Is Wilde still jealous?

P.S.S. The man who stole your heart is a fool.

~~~

Dear Alexander,

A risk you will have to take. I shall be ready tomorrow afternoon for our walk.

I am excited to hear your news.

Sophia

P.S. Don't forget the bread crumbs for the ducks.
P.S.S. No, he isn't. I gave it to him freely.

~~~

Sheffield chuckled as he read her latest note. She was a delight. He never noticed this playful side to Lady Sophia before. The lady held many facets he wished to explore. Were his feelings for Violet fading for Lady Sophia? Lady Sophia struck a chord in his lost soul filling it with humor and laughter. She also discussed intimate thoughts he would never broach with the likes of Wildeburg.

Sheffield took Sophia's advice and contacted Violet. He awaited her response. He needed to see if his feelings for her remained strong. If not, he decided he would court Lady Sophia. If he won her over before her father returned home, then the man couldn't ruin him. Sheffield knew he abused their newfound friendship with a devious agenda, but he was a desperate man. Desperate men took desperate measures. Either way he would walk away victorious. Both women held agreeable charms in their own right.

Chapter Eighteen

Sophia sipped her tea as Sidney chatted warmly with Lady Ratcliff. Sidney's newfound love for romance novels sparked a conversation with the elderly woman. At one time, Sidney only ridiculed the novels Sophia loved. However, her husband wooed her with a romance novel, and now Sidney openly discussed them as if they were works of Shakespeare. Sophia wished her conversation with Lady Dallis was going as smoothly. Instead, they sat in awkward silence. Sophia knew Lady Dallis was no longer a threat to winning Sheffield's attentions. However, the look she kept receiving was lethal. Sophia thought she would attempt again to draw Dallis out, and that perhaps she was shy.

"Did you enjoy your walk with the Duke of Sheffield?"

"Yes, he was a perfect gentleman."

"Pfft, yet she wants to throw him over for a penniless earl," her grandmother muttered.

"Nanna," Dallis hissed.

"You don't wish for Sheffield to court you?" Sidney asked Dallis.

"Why so surprised? You didn't."

"Dallis, your manners. These ladies are guests in our home, treat them with the respect they are due."

Dallis pursed her lips at her grandmother's reprimand. It was difficult to sit across from Lady Sophia with her gorgeous blonde hair and amazing color of eyes. They were the most unusual shade of purple. Violet? Was she Sheffield's mystery woman? Impossible, a lady with such a high esteem would never dally in private with a duke. Would she? Perhaps under her warm facade, she was a harlot. Lord Beckwith was enamored with her, and they displayed an affectionate embrace in the open.

Dallis's eyes narrowed more as Sophia's face expressed glee from her grandmother's comment.

Sophia sat forward in her seat. "Would the penniless earl be Lord Roderick Beckwith?"

"Yes, that is the bounder who has entranced my gel. He has her dreaming silly thoughts of them together. I've informed Dallis that he is only after her money, but she insists he is a perfect gentleman. Huh, no such thing exists. In my days men like him were scoundrels of the worst order."

"You are mistaken, Lady Ratcliff. Rory is a good man." Sophia said.

"Are you taken with him yourself, my lady?" Dallis asked.

Sidney and Sophia laughed at the absurd question. If only Dallis knew how silly her inquiry was. Sophia's heart was so entangled with Sheffield, no man could ever compare to him.

"Only as a dear friend. Rory is like a brother to me."

"I do not understand. I witnessed your affections for one another in the park yesterday."

"He was comforting me. I only laid my head on his shoulder."

"And he wrapped his arm around you."

"In a brotherly gesture. We are only friends, I assure you. His attention is drawn elsewhere."

"Oh." Although Lady Sophia had cleared the air concerning her relationship with Lord Beckwith, still, another lady held Rory's interest.

"To you, Lady Dallis," Sophia added.

"Me?"

"Yes, he is infatuated with you."

"Oh."

After they cleared her confusion, Dallis looked closer at Lady Sophia, who smiled wistfully in her direction. Dallis searched her eyes. Yes, they were definitely violet. A rare eye color. She must be Sheffield's Violet. The more she stared into her eyes, Dallis noticed the sadness lurking underneath. The mystery of their relationship was intriguing. As Sheffield's newest friend Dallis respected their privacy and would not inquire. It took all her effort to tame her curiosity.

Sidney said, "I am aware of the lateness of the invitation, but I hoped you and your granddaughter can join us for a small dinner party tomorrow evening at my home."

"Who is attending?"

"Grandmother, now you are the one displaying poor manners."

"Well?"

Sidney laughed. "Let me see, for starters, the Duke of Sheffield, Lord Beckwith, Lady Sophia, and a few other individuals."

"Humph, so you want Dallis to be the bait between the duke and the earl?"

"That is not my intention, Lady Ratcliff. I require two more ladies and I know Lady Dallis is new to society. We wish to befriend her. However, if I have offended your sensibilities with the invitation, then I will rescind."

"You didn't offend me. We will be there."

"Excellent, we shall enjoy your company. Thank you for the tea, it has been most informative."

Sidney and Sophia rose and left the Ratcliff's townhome. Their plan was falling into place. They collapsed into a fit of giggles in the carriage.

Now that they had their answers regarding Lady Dallis, Sophia needed one more thing.

To meet Sheffield one last time as Violet.

~~~~~~

Sheffield paced the room, constantly looking out the window for any sign of her arrival. She was late. After his walk with Lady Sophia he was nervous to see Violet again. Would he feel the instant attraction toward her? Was he in love or was it only lust? His feelings were conflicted, while he knew Violet owned his heart, he'd started to develop tenderness toward Sophia. He tried to remember Violet's husky laughter and her purple eyes, but all he thought about was Sophia's giggles at the ducks and her teasing. She *teased* him—a duke. Her behavior should have appalled him, instead it endeared her to him. The two women played havoc with his mind.

Throughout the walk, Sophia encouraged him to pour his soul out to Violet. To declare his true intentions. If Violet refused, then she wasn't the lady who should have possession of his heart. If Violet agreed, then he must be open to her identity and not be furious at her betrayal. Was their love strong enough to endure the secrets they kept from each other?

When he heard the door open, he turned. Violet stood inside the bedroom with a mask adorning her face as usual. Her unbound hair lay in waves down her back. She wore a simple lavender day-dress with white lace sewn into the cuffs of her sleeves. His necklace hung between her bosom. His heart stopped and had yet to begin again. He missed her. All his questions on the depth of his feelings were answered when she gifted him with a smile. Finally, he felt the familiar beat of his heart as he was drawn to Violet's side. Her mask would not discourage him.

Sophia waited for Sheffield to respond to her appearance. The longer he stood across the room, the more nervous she became. Did he love her? Was his love enough to bare her soul to him? While she had only just seen him yesterday on their walk, she couldn't look away. Yesterday, he'd visited with his friend Sophia, today he waited for Violet. The passion flaming in his eyes drew her to him. She took a step, but before Sophia could take another, he wrapped her in an embrace.

His arms swept her to him as his lips brushed across hers. With a groan, he devoured her mouth in a passionate kiss. They clung to each other as their passion exploded, their tongues dancing. He tasted of his usual whiskey. A flavor Sophia craved. She pulled his head closer wanting more. During the last couple of days, she had fallen deeper in love with Alex. She ached for him.

God, he ached for her. She was heaven and hell in his arms. He wanted to strip her naked and make love to her for hours, but he couldn't. First, he needed to earn her trust by revealing her identity. He didn't care who she was, only that he loved her, and they could work through their problems together. Before he made love to her again, he would know her name. Even though she would always be Violet to him.

She needed to touch him. Sophia started to undo his cravat, but his hand reached out to stop her. Her confused gaze met his. The desire in his eyes matched what she felt; however, a determination overshadowed his need. His need to discover who was behind the mask. Sophia hoped to make love before she took off her disguise. He brought her hand to his lips and placed soft kisses on her trembling fingers.

"Violet, we must talk."

She pulled away, walking over to the window. Sophia tried to calm her beating heart.

She said, "I swore, when I left you, to walk away. But when your letter arrived, the need to see you caused my doubts to vanish."

"You have never left my mind or my heart."

"I am in your heart?"

"You have my heart, love."

"Love?"

"Yes, I love you, Violet."

Sophia wrapped her arms around herself. He loved Violet. But would he ever love Sophia? She wanted to try a small experiment.

"Do you believe a man can love two different women who are the same?"

"Why are you talking in riddles? Did you not hear me declare my love for you?"

"You love Violet. But will you love me?"

"I love all of you. No matter who you are."

"Tell me Sheffield, how is your courtship with Lady Dallis coming along?"

"There is no courtship with Lady Dallis. We have both agreed we are not compatible."

"A shame. Who will be your next conquest? The lovely Lady Sophia?"

"Who are you?" he snarled.

Sheffield's anger grew toward Violet. She knew too much about him, and he knew nothing about her. How was she aware of his time with Sophia? They spent most of their relationship through correspondence. His eyes narrowed—she'd never mentioned if she loved him. Was he only a pawn in her game of seduction? Did she mean to trap him all along? There was an edge to her voice he never heard before. When she still didn't answer, he asked the question that weighed on his mind.

"Do you love me?"

Before she could answer, Belle rushed into the bedroom. She went to Violet's side and abruptly ushered her from the room. Belle's flustered behavior held a look of fear. He started to follow them when Ned stopped him and blocked his exit. He scowled and tried to push past the bodyguard, only to be shoved back inside. Ned slammed the door in his face. When he tried to push it back open, it wouldn't budge. Sheffield pounded his fist on the door, yelling for Violet.

He swung around and stalked to the window where he saw Violet running along the path in the garden to the carriage waiting in the alleyway. Where the hell was she going? They were not finished here. As the carriage rode past the window, he noticed the coat of arms. They were the arms belonging to Wildeburg. Wilde? Why would Violet rush away in Wilde's carriage? Unless ...

Violet was Lady Sophia Turlington. His new friend was his lover. The similarities in their personalities, their resemblance, and the taste of her kiss were obvious now. It had stared him in the face the entire time. He recalled a letter she wrote encouraging him to find his love. She signed the letter *Yours Sophia*. He was a fool. How? Why? Only questions she could answer, and she would. Tonight. The Wildeburgs were hosting a dinner this evening, and he was to be their guest. He would continue to play along with her deceit. Tonight, he would cause a scandal even Sophia could not escape.

~~~~~~

"You must leave. Wilde is waiting for you in his carriage."

"I cannot leave Alex now."

"There is no time, Wilde will explain."

Sophia didn't argue with Belle. The woman was in distress, and Sophia didn't wish to cause her any harm by remaining. She would have only interrupted them if it was important. Belle risked her business by allowing Sheffield and Violet their time together. Sophia didn't want to be the reason for any trouble.

"I understand. Thank you, Belle, for everything you have done. I will no longer ask you to risk your home again."

"You can return later; you must leave now. Sheffield can wait, and I will try to explain your reason for leaving."

"No, please do not say a word to him. Only inform him that Violet no longer exists. Tonight, I will confess who I am."

"Good luck, Sophia."

Sophia hugged Belle and undid her mask. "Give him this as a reminder of our time together."

She ran to the carriage and they swiftly departed. Wildeburg sat across from her wearing a stern expression. She'd abused his friendship and endangered their reputations. She apologized to him.

"You think I give two figs on gossip, Phee? My concern lies with the scandal you have involved yourself in."

"Why have you called me away from Belle's?"

"Your parents have returned home, and your mother is livid that you are not residing at Lord and Lady Hartridge's as per their instructions. Did you forget to inform my wife of where you were to stay? Your mother is accusing my wife and I of leading you down our path of ruination. By a thin thread I am holding my anger at the words your mother spoke degrading my wife. Sidney as usual is laughing it off and is now more than ever encouraged to continue this madness. I, on the other hand, am not. This ends this evening after dinner."

"I agree, Wilde."

"You also agreed you would not see him anymore. Sidney told me about your walk in the park and now I am gathering you from Belle's. What were you thinking?"

Sophia shrugged. "I am in love."

Wilde growled wanting to say more, but the carriage arrived at the Hartridge's townhome. When they entered the house, it was to find it in an uproar. Her mother declaring scandal, while her father rested in a chair shaking his head at her mother's rant. When his eyes met Sophia's, her father saw that his wife wasn't far off her remarks. He sighed and reached for her hand. Sophia ran and knelt at his side, laying her head on his lap.

"Do you love him?" he whispered.

"Yes, Papa." She looked up into his eyes.

"Very well. Who is he?"

"I cannot tell you yet."

"Your mother will not relent, my dear."

"Give me this evening, then I will confess all."

"Very well, I am tired from our journey. I will convince your mother to return home. You will gather your belongings from Sidney's and come home too. In the morning we will talk."

"Yes, Papa."

"Cora, stop your harping. Henry and Franny, I am sorry for the interruption and the miscommunication. It appears Sophia has resided with Sidney because of missing her friend. We are returning home. Come, my dear."

Sophia's mother said, "Sophia, express your apologies for the worry and say your farewells."

Her father quickly explained, "She will return with the Wildeburg's to attend their dinner party and will come home after breakfast tomorrow. At that time, she will explain herself."

Lord Turlington ushered his wife to their carriage. The rest of the occupants in the room breathed a sigh of relief from the drama. Sophia winced at the abuse they must have suffered because of her secrets. Her mother could be a dragon when she suspected any sign of a scandal.

Sidney's parents left the parlor, and Wilde gave Sidney a kiss and told her he would await them in the carriage.

"Sorry, Sid."

Sidney laughed. "I haven't had that much fun in ages. Your mama was breathing fire. The house was in a panic until I explained you had been staying with us the entire time. Still, she wouldn't calm down. Your mother demanded to know why you were not with me. I sent Wilde for you immediately and pacified them with half-truths until you arrived."

"Thank you."

"Well ...?"

Sophia shook her head. "No, Belle interrupted us."

"Then on to plan B."

"Which is?"

Sid laughed. "You shall see."

It didn't matter what Sidney planned. For by the end of the evening she would confess her secrets to Alex. He either loved her as Sophia or not at all.

Chapter Nineteen

The guests mingled in the library, laughing at the twist in this evening's plans. When they'd arrived, the servants handed out masks and informed them it would be a masquerade dinner. Most of the gentlemen groaned, but the ladies loved the mystery. Each of them adopted the disguises and entered the library which was filled with decorations involving characters from novels.

Sheffield leaned on the fireplace mantle as he nursed his drink. Waiting. She had yet to make her appearance, but she would. When she did, he would expose Sophia for the liar she was. Her innocent acts of wanting to avoid scandal, he now saw as ploys to trap him. When he returned home, he'd reread her letters and found the hidden lies between the lines.

He knew the moment she arrived. He felt her presence deep inside his soul. Sheffield fought the pull to glance her way. He wouldn't give her the attention she sought. He walked over to Lady Dallis and raised her hand to his mouth placing a kiss. He expected his new friend to greet him with more enthusiasm. Instead, she tried to draw her hand away and glanced around the room, but he held on.

"Sheffield," she hissed.

"Yes, my dear." He spoke loud enough for the other guests to notice.

She tugged until he released her hand. "Stop, this instant."

"Stop admiring how lovely you look this evening? Never."

Dallis didn't want to be in the middle of Sheffield and Lady's Sophia's weird courtship, no matter how much her curiosity wanted to be satisfied. Sheffield's charm delivered the wrong message to the man she truly wished to be with. Dallis noticed Lord Beckwith as soon as she entered the room. No mask could disguise him. Her eyes never strayed from him and his from hers. Now he glared in their direction. Sheffield was ruining any chance she might have with Lord Beckwith. She must make Sheffield see reason and move away from her. She needed to guide him toward Lady Sophia.

"I know who your Violet may be."

"I already know. This afternoon I uncovered the mystery surrounding her identity."

"Then why this display of affection toward me?"

"Because I have changed my mind. I no longer desire to make her my duchess."

Before Dallis could question Sheffield further, the clinking of a glass interrupted them.

"Ladies and gentlemen, dinner is served. Since we are in disguises, we will not abide by etiquette rules. Gentlemen, please escort the lady nearest to you into the dining room."

Sheffield offered his arm to Lady Dallis. When he turned them toward the door, Lady Sophia stunned him. She stood behind him waiting for him to notice her, head held high. The fragrance he gave her invaded his senses. She was exquisite. Her long blonde hair streamed along her back with curls dangling near her breasts. Her dress was a dark violet which displayed her body in a sensual nature. The fabric was cut low to tease him with a view of her breasts. Breasts he remembered only so well. His body stirred as he imagined teasing her nipples with his mouth. As his eyes rose, he saw his necklace around her neck. The amethyst twinkled in the candlelight, reminding him of why he gave her the gift.

His eyes continued to rise until they encountered hers. As usual they were behind a mask, however now he knew his Violet to be Lady Sophia Turlington. Her eyes held the look of hope. With a need to hurt her, he walked past her without any form of acknowledgement. As he did, tears welled in her depths. The sense of satisfaction he wanted to feel was not as gratifying as he thought it might be. Instead he ached for causing her pain. He pressed the emotion to the bottom of his heart as he proceeded into the dining room.

When Rory offered his arm and they followed Sheffield and Dallis, Sophia felt how tense Rory held himself. Any other time, she would offer him words of encouragement. However, her heart bled. Alex ignored her at first, then looked as if the sight of her disgusted him. She'd dressed to please him by wearing the dark violet dress and the necklace. She hoped for any sign of recognition. As they entered the dining room, she noticed Sidney place them side by side. Rory made his way around the table to sit next to Lady Dallis. The delight on the young lady's face when Rory sat made up for the cold shoulder of her dinner companion. Soon Rory turned to Dallis, and the young girl blushed at his attentions. Sheffield continued to ignore Sophia. Instead he talked to Lady Ratcliff.

On her right sat Lord Holdenburg. She only knew of him by his reputation, they'd never been formally introduced. Sophia noticed him leering down the front of her dress. Sophia also smelt the alcohol wafting off his breath. He leaned closer, causing Sophia to retreat to the side, brushing against Sheffield. He turned with a cold stare when she disturbed him.

Sheffield noticed Lord Holdenburg ogling Sophia and saw her discomfort. With his anger consuming him, he leaned across to whisper advice to the lord.

"I hear she favors whiskey over gin."

Sophia gasped at Sheffield's words. How dare he? When she caught his eye, he arched them urging her to deny his accusation. He knew. She didn't fool him. When did he guess? Now he was furious for not discovering her identity while she was Violet. Sophia was unsure how far he would play this game. Well, two could play, Sheffield. Nobody else recognized her in this room. She decided to push Sheffield to a new level of anger.

"At one time, Lord Holdenburg. However, after tonight gin might be a new flavor I enjoy." Sophia grabbed his glass and took a sip. She wanted to gag from the awful drink, but restrained herself. Her tongue traced her lips and she softly moaned with pleasure.

Lord Holdenburg eyes widened at the shameful display. Ever since Wilde married Sidney, Holdenburg held the title of the worst scoundrel of the ton. He was attractive and charming. But also a gambler and a drunk. Still, Sophia decided he would do for tonight. Sidney's Plan B would not work, so Sophia needed to improvise to Plan C. It entailed making Sheffield so jealous he would beg at her feet for her love. She noticed Sheffield's hand tightened into a fist on the table. He was not as immune as he displayed.

"What is your name, beautiful?"

"You may call me Violet," she told Lord Holdenburg, staring into Sheffield's eyes.

"Violet." Her name purred from his lips.

Sheffield blazed a fury into Sophia's eyes. Violet was *his* name for her, nobody else's. How dare she sully their time together by letting that reprobate utter her name? She arched her eyebrow at him, daring him to object. She wanted to play. Well, let's play, Lady Sophia.

"A bit more advice, Lord Holdenburg. Violet enjoys many pleasures."

"Is this knowledge from your own experiences with the exquisite Violet?"

"A gentleman does not tell."

"As if you have ever been a gentleman, Your Grace," Sophia gritted between her teeth.

Soon all conversations ceased as Wildeburg welcomed his guests into his home. After a toast to his new bride, the servants served the first course. Sophia fumed in her seat at the audacity of Sheffield's innuendo to Lord Holdenburg. She wanted to see if he was as cruel as his words, or if she still held an effect on him. She lowered her hand to her lap, pretending to fuss with her napkin, and spread her fingers across Sheffield's thigh, slowly caressing higher. She smiled as his body tensed. He didn't pull her hand away, so she raised the stakes, brushing across his cock, then away again. When her hand wandered back, it was to find him hard for her. With a few caresses, his hiss whispered past her ears, and she knew he still enjoyed her touch.

His body overruled his mind at her caress. He craved her touch. At first, he wanted to see how far she planned to test his patience. However, when her hand swept across his cock, all thoughts of fury fled his mind. As she continued to caress him, Sheffield couldn't control himself. He was hard for her and desired more than her fingers on him. When she attempted to draw her hand away, he caught it and held tight. She couldn't tug against him without bringing attention to herself. She'd thought to torture him with her touch. Well then, she could finish. He guided their strokes. A blush spread across Sophia's cheeks and Sheffield smiled as she squirmed in her seat. He'd turned her power-play against her. Did sweet Sophia imagine she could compete against him? When her eyes pleaded with him to let her go, his heart gave in. He released her trembling hand, laying it back on her lap. His eyes sent a message to cease her attack. The message she returned to him was never.

Sophia read the message in his gaze. She could no longer stop trying to win his love than she could stop loving him. He'd turned her strategy on her, however it only proved her point. He still wanted her. His cock grew hard underneath their strokes, displaying his need. When the servants brought the dessert in Sophia's eyes flew to Sidney. Her devious smile urged Sophia to tempt Sheffield until he caved.

The lemon concoction rested in front of him. The devilish minx thought a simple dessert would entice him. Ahh, she had much to learn. He was stronger than she thought. Sure, the dessert brought forth memories he would reminisce on for the rest of his life. But it would not deter him from exposing her secrets. He would ruin her tonight, so that no man would ever want her. Including himself.

Sophia remembered the last time she'd tasted this wonderful treat. It was their final night together. He'd licked the dessert off every inch of her body. She trembled from the memories. She dipped her spoon into the lemon treat, brought the pudding to her lips and moaned her delight. It came out more sensual than she meant. She sensed the other guest's eyes on her, but Sophia no longer cared. She only wanted Sheffield's gaze on her as she ate the dessert. And they were. She felt them drilling into her. Sophia took another bite, savoring the tartness on her tongue. A bit of cream stuck to her lips.

Her tongue slid along her upper lip. If he was hard before, he ached now. Her moans after every bite aroused him. And when she licked the cream away, it took everything in him to not throw Sophia over his shoulder and find somewhere private to make love.

"Your Grace, do you not like your dessert?" she asked with innocent eyes.

It was time this game ended; he no longer wanted to play. "Only when I have licked it from your body have I ever enjoyed lemon pudding as much, Lady Sophia."

The room fell silent. The game was over.

Lord Holdenburg, who was beyond drunk, didn't understand the severity of the situation. "Are you saying, my good man, this exquisite creature Violet is the lovely Lady Sophia Turlington?"

Sheffield didn't answer him, his gaze trapped in Sophia's. The shock on her face punched him in the gut. He'd meant to hurt her as deeply as he could, to cause her the same pain he felt at her deception. However, after the words spilled from his mouth, he regretted them. He understood then that her game tonight was in innocence, while his intended ruination. Damn. She always wanted to avoid scandal, and he threw her into it. The implications would impact her for the rest of her life, while he would remain unscathed. He called himself a bastard as his hand reached out to her. She shirked from his touch, a horror in her eyes he would never forget.

Sophia calmly rose from her seat and laid her napkin on the table. With her head held high, she untied her mask and let it drift into Sheffield's lap. She heard the gasps as she revealed her identity. Sophia no longer cared. He'd proved to her this evening to be the ass he always was. She'd hoped he would be Alex, only to be crushed by his cruelty as Sheffield. She turned and walked out of the dining room. Once she hit the hallway, her feet led Sophia to the garden to hide in the dark with her pain.

Every set of eyes at the dinner table were fastened on Sheffield. Nobody moved. He stared at the mask in his lap, remembering how her violet stare filled with tears as he ruined her. She didn't shed them, instead holding her head high and leaving the room as the duchess she was meant to be. During their week together, she'd hidden behind a mask only to discover a passion that frightened her. He'd worn no mask, but had been blind to the love she gifted him.

"Sheffield, leave my house now." Sidney demanded.

"I am..."

Wilde rose and came to Sheffield's side, pulling him from the chair. He recognized the tone in his wife's voice to know that if Sheffield didn't leave, she would commit murder. He pulled his friend along into the garden and shoved him on a bench.

"What in the hell were you thinking?"

Sheffield couldn't answer him. He *didn't* think of the consequences of his actions, that was the problem. He only wanted to hurt her to the same degree he hurt. Instead, he crushed Sophia. Where did she run off to? He must fix his stupidity.

"Where did she go?"

"No, you will never see her again."

"I must, I have to tell Sophia I love her."

"Love? Those were not the actions of a man in love."

"I was a fool."

"Fool doesn't even begin to describe you, Sheffield. I am the fool, I convinced myself this charade would end with you discovering the gem Sophia is. I wanted you to find the same love with her that I share with Sidney. Instead, you proved to be the same cold-hearted bastard you have always been."

Sheffield didn't argue with Wilde, for his friend spoke the truth.

"Leave before Sidney realizes you are still here. She will be on the warpath for you."

Sheffield remained in the darkened garden, his heart too heavy to leave. He dropped his head into his hands, his mind in a whirl on how to find Sophia and beg for her love. As he stared at the gravel, he saw her necklace lying between the tiny rocks. When he lifted the locket, he noticed the broken chain. If he stepped foot in Lord Turlington's home, her father would kill him and Lady Turlington would serve his head on a platter.

A wave of her perfume drifted past Sheffield. She was near.

"Sophia?"

"Sophia, please answer me."

Silence

"Please, my love, I want to hold you. Beg at your feet for forgiveness. I was an uncaring fool to embroil you in a scandal. Sophia, I love you, darling. I have been a bastard with my anger. This afternoon at Belle's, I figured out and was furious you fooled me. I came tonight to destroy you. And I did, but when I succeeded, my heart broke right alongside yours. Your pain and agony invaded my soul and is gripping tight. I want to wrap you in my embrace while you cry your heartache. When you finish crying, I will take your punches in stride. Please Sophia, answer me."

Silent tears streamed down Sophia's cheeks. Her heart ached with an unbearable sadness. While his words tempted her, she couldn't stop remembering the hatred in his eyes when he revealed her identity. He'd meant to destroy her, and she didn't know if she could trust his words now. She loved him, but he hurt her more deeply than she could allow. Also, he spoke of love. Did he understand what love meant? When you loved somebody, you don't set out to hurt them. You may hurt them unintentionally, but you never mean to destroy them.

He'd destroyed her with his hatred.

Her silence spoke her words. Sheffield had taken her beautiful affection and ruined it. He would leave her for now, but not forever. He had done enough damage for tonight. When tomorrow came, he would try to endure to win her love.

"Goodnight, my love."

Chapter Twenty

For a week, Sophia endured her mother's rants and her father's disappointment. Adding to the drama in her home, Sheffield attempted multiple times every day to see her. Poor Harry had to send him away with her denials, if not from Sophia, then from her parents. Today her father threatened to shoot him with his hunting gun, and he even sent a footman to collect the rifle from the estate. It never wavered Sheffield's determination for a chance to plead his case.

Her mother begged for her husband to accede. She decided if Sophia could wed a duke, then all talk of scandal would vanish. However, her father held a vendetta toward Sheffield that extended past the ruination of his only child. Sophia only wanted to run away and forget she ever gave her heart to him. Her body was numb, her mind empty, her soul in agony, and her heart broken in a million tiny pieces. Sophia only ate when her mother forced her. Sleep only came when exhaustion took hold—only for her to awaken in tears.

When Sophia ventured outside for the first time in days, she had to sneak away from her mother who either watched like a hawk or insisted a maid guard her. The maid sympathized and helped Sophia to escape. A footman stood near the trees, keeping an eye on her while Sophia sat watching the ducks in the pond.

A sack landed in her lap. Sophia smiled, shifting to thank Rory for the breadcrumbs she forgot. Instead it wasn't Rory, but Sheffield. Or a man she thought to be Sheffield, for he didn't hold the appearance of an ever-proper duke, but of a man who lived in hell.

His hair stood in disarray, his face covered in whiskers. The clothes were a disheveled mess. He wore no vest or cravat, and his shirt was untucked from his trousers. His suit jacket appeared as if he slept in it, every inch of the garment wrinkled beyond repair. Sophia noticed two different-colored boots, one brown and one black. When she raised her eyes to encounter his, it was to find his gaze filled with fear. Not only fear, but a desperate heartache that pulled at her.

"Alex?"

"Sophia, I ..."

"What are you doing here?"

"I had to see you."

"No." She rose, looking around for anybody to rescue her.

"I sent him home. Please talk with me, Phee."

"No, you lost all right to address me as Phee." She held up her hand, backing away.

He took a few steps toward her. "Sophia."

"Stop. I can't think when you are near."

"Don't think, just feel."

"It hurts too badly."

"I ache for you, Sophia. Let me ease your pain."

"You are the one who caused me this heartache."

"I am a fool."

"You will hear no arguments from me. Leave, Sheffield. I never want to see you again."

"I cannot leave you, Sophia Turlington, you are the other half of my soul."

"No."

His words hurt too deeply. Sophia backed away from him again before she did something as foolish as touch him. His ragged appearance worried her. When all she wanted to feel was hatred toward him for his cruel actions, one look at him and she wanted to take care of him. She wanted to kiss away the pain in his eyes. Wanted to touch him to soothe her soul. Wanted to be held by him to feel safe in their love. Were his actions part of the game he played? Sidney said he liked to play games with people's emotions.

Her foot struck a tree root causing her to fall backward. The bag spilled out of her hands. The breadcrumbs sprinkled around her when she fell, a few landing in her skirts. The ducks quickly surrounded her, fighting to eat. When they attacked her legs, Sheffield scooped Sophia off the ground and into his arms to rescue her from the small creatures.

The sensation of holding her was heaven. But when she started to cry, it turned to hell. He carried her to the bench in the gazebo for privacy. She cried into his shirt. He untied her bonnet and stroked her hair as he murmured soothing words. Which only made her cry harder. He was at a loss; his heart stalled from a fear that he'd pushed her too far. Sophia would never forgive him.

When he'd seen Sophia sitting all alone in the park, Sheffield hurried to the nearest house and begged for a sack of breadcrumbs. The cook took pity on him, assuming he was a beggar, and told him to return after dinner for meal scraps too. Sheffield rushed back to the park, hoping she would still be here. When Sophia refused to speak with him, he fell into a deeper despair. Now as she cried, he wanted to cry with her. Her pain consumed him. After a while, her tears subsided with a couple of hiccups.

He raised her head and brushed his thumbs across the drops, wiping them from her cheeks. She lifted her violet eyes to his full of sadness. He reacted the only way he knew how and brushed his mouth softly across hers. His lips slow and gentle as he caressed her lips. She stilled, but didn't pull away. He slid his tongue across her lips as he teased her mouth to open for him. When she did, he wanted to sigh. Instead he kissed her deeply, slowly, drawing out one kiss into another. So slow and tender, making her feel cherished. For that was his greatest wish; to cherish her as the love of his life.

When he lifted his head, he stared into her eyes, neither of them glancing away.

"I am sorry, my love."

"You hurt me."

"A pain I feel in my soul and will work every day for the rest of our lives to heal."

"Why?"

"I assumed you played me for a fool. You are not aware of it, but your father has threatened me with a document that could strip the dukedom from my family. I thought perhaps you were a ploy in his game. Then when you befriended me as Sophia, knowing how I cared about Violet and playing on my love for her, I felt manipulated."

Sophia smoothed the creases around his mouth, wanting to wipe away his frown. She wasn't an innocent in this mess. In her own way, she did play him. All along she held knowledge of his identity, while he didn't discover hers until the end.

"I am sorry too."

"You have nothing to apologize for."

"I fooled you because I feared you would not want me, if you figured that the Violet you desired was Sophia Turlington."

"We haven't started off on the right foot, have we?"

"You hated me."

Sheffield laughed, feeling lighter. "I believe that is the other way around, my dear."

"How so? You were always cruel to me. Both times after you kissed me, you spoke such hateful words."

"Because my dear, I knew who you were and even then, you threw me for a loop. Your kisses aroused me, and I thought the allure of your attraction would trap me. I figured if I was hateful, you would keep your distance and not tempt me into fulfilling my desires. But after Violet left and I saw you at the soiree, I couldn't take my eyes off you. You gave me doubts on my feelings toward Violet."

"So, you wanted both of us?"

"Yes, and I fought the conflict. But then I didn't need to, did I? For you two are one and the same, and knowing that I became furious at myself. Because all the signs were there and I refused to notice them. So, I blamed you for making me a fool."

"Do you forgive me?"

"Ah, Sophia, I forgave you the minute I hurt you. I only hope one day you can forgive me."

"I forgive you, Sheffield."

"Alex, my Sophia."

"Alexander."

"Am I forgiven enough that you will agree to be my duchess?"

"I am not aware you have asked me."

"Sophia, my dearest, I love you with all my heart. Will you do me the honor of becoming my bride?"

"Do you love me or are you in love with Violet? I am not her; I am Sophia."

"Are you not, my dear? I fear you are wrong. Violet is the woman you have always desired to be but held yourself back from becoming so as not to disappoint anyone. I love you as Sophia *and* as Violet. As my wife, I hope you will allow Violet into your world of being Sophia. Because they are both beautiful creatures who carry my heart."

Sophia started to cry again at his sweet words. He understood her better than she did herself. How did she ever think him to be a man of an overbearing nature? He was the dearest man on earth, and she promised to make him feel special every day.

"I love you, Alex. Your love inspires me. I would love to be your bride."

Sophia lifted her head to seal her promise with a kiss. Her fingers slid around his neck deepening the kiss, wanting to show him her love and forgiveness. Their kiss turned passionate as they expressed their desires and happiness. Soon Alex's hands roamed her body, caressing as Sophia moaned her delight. Lost in the passion of each other, they forgot they were in a park. When a couple of ladies walked by expressing their disgust at such a vulgar display of affection, Sophia and Alex fell into a fit of laughter. When the ladies noticed who they were, and the scandal attached to them, they rushed away.

"I fear, my dear, we are ruined."

"Yes, my love, it appears so. Kiss me again before you take me home. If we hurry, you should be safe from Papa's gun."

"What?"

"Never mind, we shall go to your place first and then send for my parents."

"Gun?"

"Kiss me, Alex," Sophia demanded.

Alex kissed Sophia long and passionate, and before long he forgot about the gun. He carried her to his carriage, kissing her along the way. The gasps and sighs as they left the park echoed around them. Once inside, he fought to keep her hands off him. He wanted her, but not inside a carriage. He wanted her spread across his sheets as he made love to her for the first time without a mask. Also, he wanted to wait until she was his bride. He would endure her father's wrath and court her as she deserved until they were married. It would frustrate him, but she would be worth the wait.

Alex confused Sophia when his carriage arrived at her parents' townhouse. From the way he caressed and kissed her, she thought Alex was taking her to his home. She couldn't enter the house appearing this disheveled. Her hair hung in tangles and his hands had wrinkled her dress. She traced the fullness of her lips from his kisses and knew her parents would be furious.

"Alex?"

"Yes, dear."

"I thought ..."

"I know—and believe me, I want to. But I also want to right my wrongs and to do that I need your parents' approval."

"My father wants to kill you."

"Kill is a strong word, my love."

"Not when it is the correct word. You do not understand."

"Come love, trust me."

Sophia allowed Alex to escort her inside. When they crossed the threshold, it was to find her father with a loaded rifle pointed at Sheffield, her mother panicking at his side. Her fire-breathing mama was in a fit of hysterics. Sophia gasped and pleaded with her father to lower the gun.

"Give me one good reason not to shoot your head off."

"I love your daughter and will cherish her for the rest of my life."

Her mother gasped, "Oh, Samuel, how romantic."

"Is this a ploy to stop me from releasing the document?"

"No. This is simply a man falling in love with a woman and wanting to create a life with her. You have my permission to expose the document for the truth it may hold."

"It will ruin you."

"I am aware of the repercussions."

"This will ruin Sophia too."

Sophia said, "I will only be ruined if I have to spend my life away from him. Whatever you hold over him, we will endure together."

"And if I forbid this union?"

"Then it will happen anyway, Father. I love him and no other."

Her father sighed. "I am outnumbered. Meet me in my study to discuss the marriage contract."

Her father walked away defeated and her mother crowed her delight at the good news. She rushed to the parlor with instructions to the servants on a wedding to plan. Sophia chuckled on how quickly a moment could change. One minute her father threatened Alex with a gun, and the next plans for their marriage were under way.

"What is so funny?"

"Life."

"Mmm, I believe you are correct."

"Will you sneak into my room after you are finished with my father?"

"No, I will return home."

"Will you meet me at Belle's?"

"No, Sophia. From this day forth, Belle's is off limits to you."

"But it is open for you, I suppose. I remember your remarks from when you courted Sidney."

Sophia's temper rose at his denial for them to be together. Now that she agreed to marry him, apparently his life would return to the normal activities of carousing while she sat at home all demure.

"No, my jealous duck. I will not be visiting Belle's again, you are enough."

"Then why?"

"Because I owe you the courtship you deserve. Our whole relationship has been unorthodox. I wish to create memories for you to cherish."

"Every memory we have shared, I will cherish. I do not need this simple nonsense, nor do I want it."

"But I do, love."

She tried to tempt him. "I want you, Alex." Her whisper turned husky as she stroked his body.

He tensed from the sound of her voice and the touch of her fingers as she caressed him. His willpower was weak to begin with and the added temptation of her seduction was more than he could handle.

"One week, and I will get a special license. Give me one week," he pleaded.

Sophia pouted. "One week."

Sheffield glanced over his shoulder to make sure they were alone and that her father didn't lurk around the corner. Then he pulled her to him and gave her a kiss full of promises to come. With a final kiss on her nose, he turned and strolled to her father's study to arrange for Sophia to be his bride.

Sophia sighed as he walked away. She would give him one week, but wouldn't make it easy on him. She planned to tempt him at every opportunity.

Chapter Twenty-One

And she didn't make it easy for him. Sophia tempted Sheffield at every turn. From the cut of her dress to the lingering touch of her hand. His need for her was undeniable. Her parents never left them alone, hovering to the point of annoyance. But through the week he charmed her mother and fixed the rift with her father, who burnt the document stating Sheffield was not the legitimate heir to the Sheffield name. Lord Hartridge had proved the document to be false and explained the forgery. They destroyed the paper so that no future generation had to deal with the dilemma. Sheffield and Sophia's father even managed to compromise on a few key topics in Parliament.

However, the letters from Sophia teased Sheffield's mind and made him crazy with need. They would range from his sweet Sophia to his temptress Violet. Each letter holding a special place in his heart.

When he replied, Sheffield also sent a gift. Little trinkets of affection, each one endearing her heart to him more. Alex was sexy, sweet, loving and a tease. Sophia's frustrations grew with being so near to him, yet so far away. Her frustration turned to a longing and a desire to be his wife after his last letter and gift. She held the letter, tears of love streaming down her face.

My darling Sophia,

You tore this from your heart with pain. I hope you wear it upon your heart today in love. I do not deserve you, but I will attempt every day to try. You tempted me as Violet, but it is you Sophia who I love. You are the temptress that captured my heart.

I love you.

Your soon to be husband,

Alexander

Sophia opened the small box. Inside was the necklace. She remembered ripping it from her throat the night he destroyed her. She had thrown it away in Sidney's garden. Her fingers trembled as she traced the purple stone in the heart, her love for him spreading through her body, eager to be his bride. She slid the necklace around her throat. The final piece to make today perfect.

As Sophia walked down the aisle, Alex stood at the front nervous for fear she would not come. When he saw the beauty of her smile radiate the church, he felt honored to have been given the gift of such a wonderful woman. When he noticed the necklace resting against her chest, he knew all was forgiven and their love would only flourish from this day forth.

Once they spoke their vows, he kissed his bride. Soon their friends and family set upon them with their congratulations. Then they enjoyed a reception at Sophia's parents' home. After many handshakes, hugs, and toasts they were able to sneak away.

Alex carried her over the threshold of his townhome, his eyes lost in hers. He waved, dismissing the servants as he carried her to his bedroom. He'd waited for this moment impatiently for over a week. Many distractions throughout that time kept them from being alone. Today he would make Sophia his true love.

Sophia lay in his arms; her gaze entranced by his. She could feel his arms tremble as he held her. She lifted her hand and held his cheek.

"I love you, Alex."

"Ahh Phee, you are my heart and soul."

"Then are you going to kiss me or not? I have been dying for the taste of your lips for an eternity."

Alex laughed. "Are you going to be a task-master, my duchess?"

"Only when my duke keeps me waiting."

So, on her orders, he lowered his head and took her lips in a kiss to make memories. Each kiss leading into another as they poured their emotions into each other's souls. As he lowered her to her feet, they slowly removed their clothing. He lifted her again and laid Sophia on his bed.

As he made love to her, his eyes never left hers. No mask covered Sophia's face. Each of them lay exposed to the other, open and vulnerable. With every kiss and stroke of his fingers he watched her full expression come alive.

Their bodies joined, clinging to each other, and whispering words of love. When he exploded inside her, his fingers traced around her eyes. Her tears gliding off his fingertips. She was beautiful to him, inside and out.

Sophia cried as they made love. The beauty of their love-making touched a deeper part of her soul. That was how it was with Alex; he drew emotions from her that Sophia didn't know she possessed.

They lay side by side and whispering into the night, her fingers wrapped around the necklace and his intertwined holding their love close. Sophia was secure and knew that Alex loved her for who she was, not who she portrayed as Violet. However, Violet brought them together and might appear from time to time. She smiled secretively at Alex, and he returned her smile, pulling her underneath him and making her dreams come true.

Her smile spoke her intentions. From the look in her eye, to the smile that graced her lips, to the touch of her fingers, he would be forever brought to his knees. His new duchess achieved what many said could never be done, but he would do for the rest of their lives together.

Epilogue

"Now that you are home from your honeymoon, you can assist me with my latest project."

"Another experiment, Sid?"

"I refer to them as matchmaking, Phee."

Sophia laughed as Sidney tried explaining the differences between the two terms. Even though the end result would be the same.

"Who is the unlucky couple?"

Sid joined Phee's laughter at her teasing. She stared at the happiness glowing off her friend. Because of her interference, Sophia was now happily married to Alexander Langley. At one time the newlyweds never got along. With a gentle push in the right direction they found their love for each other. All as a result from her matchmaking attempts. It was the least she could do, since Phee helped her with Wilde. Now all Sidney wanted was to help their friend and she would need Phee's assistance.

"Rory and Lady Dallis MacPherson."

"Sid, I think you should leave well enough alone with Rory. He will not take kindly to our meddling."

"He doesn't have to know, Phee. We will just nudge him discreetly in her direction. He is infatuated with her, and you heard how she is interested in him. They are a perfect match."

"You are forgetting the main factor."

"And that is?"

"He is broke, and her grandfather will only allow her to marry a man of wealth and power. Sadly to say, our friend has neither."

Sidney waved this away. "A small matter of unimportance. Love conquers all. Why, just the other day, I read this novel about an impoverished duke who loved an heiress. Her father never approved, but the duke whisked her away to Scotland and married her. Their passion overruled common sense as they discovered their deep, abiding love. Rory and Dallis only need to discover the same."

Sophia rolled her eyes. Now that Sidney was obsessed with love stories, her friend thought everyone needed to find their happily ever after.

"What do Rory and Dallis need to discover?"

Alex and Wilde strode inside the parlor, catching the end of Sidney's declaration for Rory. Alex only had eyes for his wife and he watched the secret smile light up her face as he came to her side. He leaned over to kiss her gently on the mouth. His lips lingered until he heard Wilde's soft cough, followed by Sidney's laughter. His desire for Sophia never diminished. Any minute spent away only grew his need stronger.

"Sidney wants to play matchmaker between Rory and Dallis. She thinks they need to discover their love for one another." Sophia explained.

"Sidney, you made a promise to leave them be," Wilde growled.

"She may be on to something," Sheffield said.

"I am?" Sidney asked.

"What?" Sophia and Wilde exclaimed.

Sheffield laughed. To be in agreement with Sidney was shocking to say the least. However, he wanted to help her. He owed Lady Dallis for his boorish behavior at the Wildeburg's dinner party. Plus, if he could make Beckwith suffer, it was all the more pleasurable.

"What do you have planned?" Sheffield asked Sidney.

Wilde rose from the couch and pulled Sidney to her feet. He would not allow this scheme to go any further. He wasn't acquainted with Lady Dallis, but he understood the devious minds of his wife and friend enough to realize this would only end in disaster. While he got along with Beckwith, he also knew of his struggles. Beckwith's pride would be his downfall for this matchmaking plan to succeed. It would seem Wilde needed to keep his wife well occupied for the rest of the season. He guided her toward the door before any more of this discussion continued.

"We shall talk later, Sheffield." Sidney laughed as Wilde ushered her away.

Sheffield laughed as he watched his friend try to handle his wife. *Try* being the operative word. When he caught Sophia's eye, she narrowed her gaze at his amusement. He lifted her into his arms and settled back on the chair with her in his lap. When he lowered his head to kiss her, she pulled away.

"You are not serious on helping Sidney, are you?"

"Perhaps, I am." He lowered his head again, this time capturing her lips in kiss.

"Alex."

Her plea went unnoticed as he continued his assault on her senses. His kisses grew bolder as passion took hold. He would never be able to get enough of her. The need for her consumed him. He slowly unbuttoned her dress, peeling it off her shoulders as his kisses slid lower.

Sophia trembled in his arms as her passion grew. He distracted her from her questions with his kisses. He couldn't be serious on helping Sidney with Rory's quest for love.

Before long she forgot what they discussed as Sheffield lifted Sophia in his arms and carried her to their bedroom.

Read Rory's story in I Shall Love the Earl

Visit my website www.lauraabarnes.com to join my mailing list.

"Thank you for reading Whom Shall I Marry... An Earl or A Duke? Gaining exposure as an independent author relies mostly on word-of-mouth, so if you have the time and inclination, please consider leaving a short review wherever you can."

Author Laura A. Barnes

International selling author Laura A. Barnes fell in love with writing in the second grade. After her first creative writing assignment, she knew what she wanted to become. Thirty-seven years later, she made her dreams a reality. With her debut novel *Rescued By the Captain*, she has set out on the path she always dreamed about.

When not writing, Laura can be found devouring her favorite romance books. Laura is married to her own Prince Charming (who for some reason or another thinks the heroes in her books are about him) and they have three wonderful children and two sweet grandbabies. Besides her love of reading and writing, Laura loves to travel.

You can visit her at www.lauraabarnes.com to join her mailing list.

Tricking the Scoundrels Series:
Whom Shall I Kiss… An Earl, A Marquess, or A Duke?
Whom Shall I Marry… An Earl or A Duke?
I Shall Love the Earl
The Scoundrel's Wager
The Forgiven Scoundrel

Romancing the Spies Series:
Rescued By the Captain
Rescued By the Spy
Rescued By the Scot

Made in the USA
Monee, IL
01 September 2020